NORTHBROOK
1201
NORTHBROOK,

W9-CIY-499

Northbrook Public Library

3 1123 01093 0413

RETURN TO CLAN SINCLAIR

TP+ HER PUBLIC LIBRARY MAR 1 7 20??
CEDAR LANE
NORTH BROOK, IL 60062

By Karen Ranney

Return to Clan Sinclair
The Virgin of Clan Sinclair
The Witch of Clan Sinclair
The Devil of Clan Sinclair
The Lass Wore Black
A Scandalous Scot
A Scottish Love
A Borrowed Scot
A Highland Duchess
Sold to a Laird
A Scotsman in Love
The Devil Wears Tartan
The Scottish Companion
Autumn in Scotland
An Unlikely Governess
Till Next We Meet
So in Love
To Love a Scottish Lord
The Irresistible MacRae
When the Laird Returns
One Man's Love
After the Kiss
My True Love
My Beloved
Upon a Wicked Time
My Wicked Fantasy

RETURN TO CLAN SINCLAIR

A Clan Sinclair Novella

KAREN RANNEY

AVONIMPULSE
An Imprint of HarperCollins Publishers

This is a work of fiction. Names, characters, places, and incidents are products of the author's imagination or are used fictitiously and are not to be construed as real. Any resemblance to actual events, locales, organizations, or persons, living or dead, is entirely coincidental.

Excerpt from *In Your Wildest Scottish Dreams* copyright © 2015 by Karen Ranney LLC.

Excerpt from *An Heiress for All Seasons* copyright © 2014 by Sharie Kohler.

Excerpt from *Intrusion* copyright © 2014 by Charlotte Stein.

Excerpt from *Can't Wait* copyright © 2013 by Jennifer Hopkins. This novella originally appeared in the anthology *All I Want for Christmas Is a Cowboy*.

Excerpt from *The Laws of Seduction* copyright © 2014 by Gwen T. Weerheim-Jones.

Excerpt from *Sinful Rewards 1* copyright © 2014 by Cynthia Sax.

Excerpt from *Sweet Cowboy Christmas* copyright © 2014 by Candis Terry.

RETURN TO CLAN SINCLAIR. Copyright © 2014 by Karen Ranney LLC. All rights reserved under International and Pan-American Copyright Conventions. By payment of the required fees, you have been granted the nonexclusive, nontransferable right to access and read the text of this e-book on screen. No part of this text may be reproduced, transmitted, decompiled, reverse-engineered, or stored in or introduced into any information storage and retrieval system, in any form or by any means, whether electronic or mechanical, now known or hereafter invented, without the express written permission of HarperCollins e-books.

EPub Edition DECEMBER 2014 ISBN: 9780062337450
Print Edition ISBN: 9780062337467

10 9 8 7 6 5 4 3 2 1

CHAPTER ONE

July, 1880
Drumvagen, Scotland

Her driver slowed to a halt, no doubt getting an eyeful of Drumvagen and the Scottish coast. Ceana would wager a goodly sum that by the time the week was out, he would have posted a report of everything to her brothers-in-law. The same intransigent, annoying, and beloved brothers-in-law who were trying to render her as dead as her poor husband, Peter.

She'd been a widow for three years now, during which they'd been her guardians. She couldn't escape them. Wherever she went, one of the three brothers was there.

"Do you need anything, Ceana?"

"Can I fetch anything from town for you?"

"Shall we order something from London?"

"You're looking a little peaked, would you like to take the sun with me?"

They'd offered their arms, their interest, their help, and their eternal interference.

So she had done what any self-respecting Scot would do when faced with three Irish brothers-in-law: she'd run away from home.

She dismounted from the carriage, standing there staring in awe.

Granted, Iverclaire was a lovely place, an enchanted castle in Ireland, quite a forbidding yet beautiful structure. But Drumvagen, this had been created by her own brother.

They'd been so poor once upon a time, but Macrath had taken his dream and made it come true. Because of him, she'd had a season in London and had married the son of a duke.

Yet she always thought she had something to do with his happiness as well. Her friendship with Virginia had led them to be introduced at numerous events. When Virginia and Macrath were finally married after her first husband died, she wasn't the least surprised.

Nor was she the least surprised when Alistair, Virginia's first child, looked just like Macrath.

The seabirds called a greeting to her, swooping down on air currents blowing the scent of the sea to her.

For days, she'd been alone in the carriage, encased in a bubble of silence. Other than speaking to the driver first thing in the morning and when they stopped for a meal, she hadn't talked to another person.

At first she'd missed her daughters terribly. Then she realized the time was her own, to think, to mull, to remember. When she went home, she'd be a better mother to Darina and Nessa.

She stood at the base of the steps, staring upward. Virginia had told her about Drumvagen, but even her description failed to convey just how impressive the house was.

Built of gray brick sparkling in the sunlight, it was four stories tall with rows of windows reflecting both the sun and the sea to her right. But most impressive of all was the twin staircase beginning at the broad front doors and curving down and around like arms reaching out to enfold her.

She took the right staircase and, with her left hand gripping her skirt, placed her right on the broad stone banister, slowly ascending the steps.

At the top, she stopped and turned and looked at the ocean. Far off in the distance was the North Sea. Drumvagen and its neighboring village, Kinloch, was the perfect place for Macrath to live. From here he could simply sail away to anyplace in the world he wished to be.

She glanced down at the carriage and her driver, standing at the head of the horses with his cap in his hand. Thomas was a good man, but he was a toady to all the Meads. He was going to tell them everything they wanted to know, which was a pity. The man had a good memory, and she'd no doubt already erred in some manner.

Her lips twitched at the brass knocker on one of the big broad doors. Macrath had evidently had the refrigeration machine's likeness made especially for Drumvagen. She picked it up and let it drop, hearing the echo in the foyer.

A moment later the door was flung open. A body slammed into her, arms gripping her waist, pulling so tightly on her dress her train almost toppled in a flurry of fabric. She found herself falling, only righting herself by gripping the door frame.

"Save me! Please! Don't let her get me!"

Ceana stared down at her niece. The poor girl was trembling and she had splotchy color on her cheeks.

"Fiona?" She reached down, enfolding the girl in a hug. "What's wrong?"

"It's Brianag, I've done something terrible and she made the sign of evil over me just like a witch. I'm going to get sick and die, I know it."

Who was this Brianag who was tormenting the poor child?

"Aunt Ceana."

She looked up at the sound of the composed voice, blinking at her nephew. Alistair was only fourteen but already had the height of his father, not to mention his demeanor.

As she stood on the doorstep, he extended his hand to her.

"How nice to see you again Aunt Ceana," he said. He glanced down at his sister dismissively. "You must pardon Fiona. She's a silly little thing."

"I am not silly. I'll tell Brianag you broke her jar of spices."

To Ceana's great surprise, Alistair paled.

"That wouldn't be well done of you, Fiona. You know as well as I do it was your carelessness that made the jar fall. Father always says we have to deal with the consequences of our actions."

"Where are your parents?" Ceana asked. "Where are Macrath and Virginia?"

"They've gone to Edinburgh, they have," a voice said. "Leaving me to deal with their spawn."

She looked up past Alistair and—God help her!—took a step back toward the steep stairs.

Fiona was more correct than she had assumed.

Drumvagen did have a witch.

The woman who met her eyes was tall and square with a face the same. She was almost masculine in appearance, a warrior like creature whose legs were braced apart and arms folded in front of her. Her nose was a formidable hawkish feature, as were her narrowed eyes and clenched jaw.

Was the woman a watchdog Macrath had put in place to guard his children in his absence? Was she going to have to fight her to advance a foot farther into Drumvagen?

"I'm Ceana Sinclair Mead," she said.

"She's my aunt," Alistair said.

Fiona moved to stand behind her.

"Aye," Brianag said, nodding. "You've got the look of the Sinclairs. It's the eyes. Devil's eyes, I call them."

Since three of the people in the foyer had the deep blue Sinclair eyes, that was hardly a polite or tactful way of describing them, but she doubted Brianag did anything remotely polite or tactful.

"I understand my brother has gone to Edinburgh," she said.

A sharp nod of the head was the only response she got.

"I've come to visit," she said, straightening her shoulders. She hadn't traveled from Ireland just to be put in her place by a Scottish terror.

Ceana looked at Alistair, standing with his arms folded,

watching the byplay between the two of them. She was determined to have the same sangfroid as her nephew.

"Have you a guest chamber at Drumvagen?" she asked him.

"I'm the housekeeper here," Brianag said.

Oh, so that was the position the Scottish terror occupied. Macrath evidently thought a great deal of her to both install her in the position and place her in charge of the children.

Where was Carlton?

"Then I suggest you act as a housekeeper," Ceana said, her voice icy. "I am Macrath Sinclair's sister and I've come a very long way. A proper housekeeper would not keep me standing in the foyer but would have been gracious and inviting. Show me to a guest chamber, direct my driver to the stable, and fetch my baggage. Afterward, you can offer me some refreshments. Some tea, perhaps, and something to eat. You would be better served doing that than terrifying children."

She took Fiona's hand, nodded at Brianag and turned to her nephew. "If you'll show me to a parlor, Alistair," she said. "I'll wait there until your the housekeeper has decided to welcome me."

And with that, she and Fiona followed Alistair through Drumvagen. She heard a sound behind her, a kind of grunt mixed with a muffled oath. One of her brothers-in-law was forever swearing, and she knew a daunting collection of Irish oaths. She didn't doubt she could be Brianag's equal in profanity.

She didn't care how annoyed the housekeeper was as long as the woman did what she asked and didn't put anything in her food.

That might be too much to wish for, however.

She followed Alistair into a room filled with Scottish fervor. The tartan of the window coverings was matched by the pillows on the emerald settee. The chairs were tartan as well, as if to remind the inhabitants of this parlor they were in Scotland.

She took one corner of the settee, not at all surprised when Fiona sat beside her. Evidently, she'd acquired the status of a female slayer of dragons by refusing to be cowed by Brianag.

"Where is Carlton?" she asked, referring to the youngest of Macrath's children.

"He's been sent to his room," Fiona said. "Papa is not happy with him."

Alistair rolled his eyes, an expression Ceana had seen Virginia make often enough that she bit back her smile.

"What did he do?"

"It's what he didn't do," Fiona said, sighing. "He rode Papa's new horse without telling anyone. He hitched the oxen to the wagon and took himself off to the village. He refused to eat something Brianag made for him. And he sassed Papa."

Well, the latter two would have gotten him gruel, no doubt.

Carlton was only a year or so younger than Fiona. Surely a ten-year-old would not be so adventurous. But then, he was Macrath's son.

"He won't stay in his room," Fiona said. "He never does."

"Well, if that happens," Alistair said, "the punishment will just be more strict. Our parents are considering sending him off to school, which won't be a good thing for Carlton. He loves Drumvagen."

"And you, Alistair? Do you go off to school?"

That would account for her nephew's almost adult demeanor.

He looked exactly like Macrath had at his age, tall and spindle thin, with black hair left longer than it should be and the piercing blue eyes marking a Sinclair. There were touches of Virginia's beauty in the young man's face, in the shape of his nose and the perfection of his cheekbones and chin. Alistair was an attractive young man. Fully grown, he would be incredibly handsome.

"I do, yes, Aunt Ceana. I'm off to England again in a matter of weeks."

"Do you like it?"

"I do," he said, to her surprise. "I'm interested in mathematics and engineering. There's no one here who can give me training other than father, and he's busy with the new invention. I want to learn as much as I can to be of help to him."

So Alistair understood he was Macrath's scion, the heir to his empire, one that was growing daily, from what she understood.

Fiona looked up at her wide-eyed. "You talked back to Brianag. Nobody ever talks back to Brianag," she said. "Not even Mama."

Alistair sent her a look, one she interpreted as, *What are you going to do about a little sister?*

Since she was Macrath's little sister, she felt some kinship with her niece.

"What did you do that made Brianag so angry?" she asked Fiona.

"Brianag wasn't all that angry," Alistair said. "She was

being rather kind." He spared a glance in his sister's direction. "Fiona was racing through the kitchen and she knows she's not allowed to run in the house."

"It was an accident," Fiona said. "I must've knocked off the jar from the table. I never even saw it until there was a mess on the floor. All of Brianag's special witchy herbs."

"She isn't a witch, Fiona. She likes people to think she is, but she isn't. She goes to church every Sunday and she gives alms to the poor. She does a lot of good works."

The image of a St. Brianag didn't quite conform to the person she'd already seen, but Ceana thought it would be better if she withheld that comment until she learned a bit more about the household.

"I should have sent word I was coming," she said, a remonstration to herself and a comment to her very adult nephew.

He smiled, an utterly charming expression, and so like Macrath she stopped for a moment, catapulted back into the past. He might have said the same words Macrath often said to her back then: *It's going to be better, Ceana, don't worry. It's going to be all right, I promise.*

They would have enough food to eat. They would have enough money to make sure they stayed warm.

He'd made good on all those promises and more. Because of Macrath, she'd had a London season with new dresses and a dance instructor. Because of Macrath, she'd married the son of a duke.

"If you'll pardon me, Aunt Ceana," Alistair said, unaware of her mental trip to Edinburgh and the days of penury, "I'll go and see what room Brianag has assigned to you."

She had the most absurd wish to apologize for her arrival.

Or causing a disagreement with the housekeeper, but she had a feeling facing Brianag down had elevated her stature in Alistair's eyes as well.

What was Macrath thinking, to allow Brianag to be in charge of the children? She chided herself for the question. What she was engaging in now was a little of her Irish brothers-in-law behavior. What right had she to dictate anything? Sweet and unassuming as Fiona appeared, there was every chance she, herself, was as much a hellion as Carlton was rumored to be.

Drumvagen was as different from Iverclaire as she'd hoped.

CHAPTER TWO

"See? I told you he wouldn't stay in his room. See? I told you," Fiona said, pointing to the window.

At first Ceana couldn't make out exactly what she was seeing: a corner of a curtain, perhaps, or a bit of laundry falling from the window. Then she realized it was a rope made of some material, perhaps sheets. As she watched, two shoes came into view, then a pair of trousers.

"He's going to the grotto."

"He's going to kill himself," Ceana said, standing and estimating the distance to the beach.

Fiona shook her head. "He's done it before."

Just then Carlton's face came into view. Her nephew grinned at her, an expression reminding her of Virginia's smile, just before he glanced down and his look changed to terror.

"Where's the grotto?" Ceana asked, her voice rough with urgency. She'd heard of Drumvagen's grotto but had never seen it. "Show me, Fiona. Now!"

Her niece slid from the settee, grabbed her hand and

pulled her from the parlor, racing down one of Drumvagen's corridors.

They came to a closed door, but Fiona opened it without hesitation, revealing a library that was probably Macrath's domain and forbidden to his children. She would have to make her apologies after she'd saved Carlton.

Fiona ran to the bookshelf.

"There's a latch up there," she said, pointing to the second shelf from the top. "Can you see it?"

She could.

"Pull it down and then pull the bookshelf out. It leads to a passage to the grotto."

She turned. "Aren't you coming, Fiona?"

The girl shook her head. "No, it's too dark."

She wasn't fond of the dark, either, or things lingering there, like bugs and snakes and vermin. But she had Carlton to think of. How horrible would it be for Macrath and Virginia to return from Edinburgh to find she'd been present at the death of their child?

The darkness was nearly absolute, leaving her no choice but to stretch her hands out on either side of her, fingertips brushing against the stone walls. The incline was steep, further necessitating she take her time. Yet at the back of her mind was the last image she had of Carlton, his bright impish grin turning to horror as he glanced down.

The passage abruptly ended in a mushroom-shaped cavern. This was the grotto she'd heard so much about, with its flue in the middle and its broad, wide window looking out over the beach and the sea. She raced to the window, hopped up on the sill nature had created over thousands of years and leaned out.

A naked man reached up, grabbed Carlton as he fell. After he lowered the boy to the sand, he turned and smiled at her.

Carlton was racing across the beach, glancing back once or twice to see if he was indeed free. The rope made of sheets was hanging limply from his window.

The naked man was standing there with hands on his hips, staring at her in full frontal glory.

She hadn't seen many naked men, the last being her husband. The image in front of her now was so startling she couldn't help but stare. A smile was dawning on the stranger's full lips, one matched by his intent brown eyes. No, not quite brown, were they? They were like the finest Scottish whiskey touched with sunlight.

Her gaze danced down his strong and corded neck to broad shoulders etched with muscle. His chest was broad and muscled as well, tapering down to a slim waist and hips.

Even semiflaccid, his manhood was quite impressive.

The longer she watched, the more impressive it became.

What on earth was a naked man doing on Macrath's beach?

To her utter chagrin, the stranger turned and presented his backside to her, glancing over his shoulder to see if she approved of the sight.

She withdrew from the window, cheeks flaming. What on earth had she been doing? Who was she to gawk at a naked man as if she'd never before seen one?

Now that she knew Carlton was going to survive his escape, she should retreat immediately to the library.

"You'd better tell Alistair his brother's gotten loose again. Are you the new governess?"

She turned to find him standing in the doorway, still naked.

She pressed her fingers against the base of her throat and counseled herself to appear unaffected.

"I warn you, the imp escapes at any chance. You'll have your hands full there."

The look of fright on Carlton's face hadn't been fear of the distance to the beach, but the fact that he'd been caught.

She couldn't quite place the man's accent, but it wasn't Scottish. American, perhaps. What did she care where he came from? The problem was what he was doing here.

"I'm not a governess," she said. "I'm Macrath's sister, Ceana."

He bent and retrieved his shirt from a pile of clothes beside the door, taking his time with it. Shouldn't he have begun with his trousers instead?

"Who are you?" she asked, looking away as he began to don the rest of his clothing.

She'd had two children. She was well versed in matters of nature. She knew quite well what a man's body looked like. The fact that his struck her as singularly attractive was no doubt due to the fact she'd been a widow for three years.

"Well, Ceana Sinclair, is it all that important you know who I am?"

"It isn't Sinclair," she said. "It's Mead."

He tilted his head and studied her.

"Is Mr. Mead visiting along with you?"

She stared down at her dress of unremitting black. "I'm a widow," she said.

A shadow flitted over his face "Are you? Did Macrath know you were coming?"

"No," she said. "Does it matter? He's my brother. He's family. And why would you be wanting to know?"

He shrugged, finished buttoning his pants and began to don his shoes.

"Who are you?" she asked again.

"I'm a detective," he said. "My company was hired by your brother."

"Why?"

"Now that's something I'm most assuredly not going to tell you," he said. "It was nice meeting you, Mrs. Mead. I hope to see more of you before I leave."

And she hoped to see much, much less of him.

She heard the conversation halfway back up to the library. To her surprise, however, the door was shut tight. At the top of the passage she fumbled in the dark for the latch, wishing she'd made note of it before descending to the grotto.

"If you move," he said directly behind her, "I'll open the door for you."

She jerked, startled by the sound of his voice so close. How had he crept up on her unaware?

"Where do you suggest I stand?" she asked.

His hands on her shoulders surprised her. She almost

brushed aside his touch, but he was trying to help, so she allowed him to guide her to the far wall.

The total darkness was disorienting. He smelled of the sea and sun-warmed skin and was entirely too close.

"There," he said, bending low, so near she could feel his breath on her forehead. "Just stand there for a moment."

"You're an American," she said.

"You sound Irish," he said. "But if you're Macrath's sister you should be a Scot."

"Would you please open the door," she said. *And move away, please.*

He chuckled as if he'd heard her unspoken words, turned and engaged a latch she still couldn't see.

The door swung open to reveal four surprised people.

Alistair evidently hadn't been told where they'd disappeared, Brianag scowled at her, and Macrath and Virginia both looked amazed as she exited the secret passage behind the stranger.

"Ceana!" Virginia reached her and, in a flurry of silk and warmth, enveloped her in an embrace. "Dearest Ceana, what on earth are you doing here and how glad I am to see you."

The second person to embrace her was her brother. He did so in such an exuberant manner, it left no doubt about his welcome.

"It's about time you came to Drumvagen," he said, stepping back. "Where are the girls?"

"I left them at Iverclaire," she said, knowing she'd have to tell him the whole story. Or tell Virginia, which was the same thing.

"Bruce," he said, reaching over to shake the hand of the stranger. "I see you've met my sister."

"She's met your youngest as well," the stranger said, laughter bubbling up in his voice. "I'm afraid I had to rescue Carlton once again. He climbed out of his window and was heading for disaster."

Virginia's hand went to her lips. "Oh no."

"Thank you," Macrath said.

"You might want to put an iron bar across the window. Or move him so that his window doesn't overlook the beach. It seems to be a temptation."

Macrath only nodded. Bruce left the room, leaving the four of them standing there. Brianag glared at all of them before she, too, departed, mumbling about uninvited guests.

"I should have sent word," Ceana said.

"Brianag is getting up in years and she's been testy of late. I apologize for the rudeness with which you were treated." He glanced toward Alistair, who evidently had told his father about her arrival. "Drumvagen is known for its hospitality, and I'm sorry you weren't shown that."

Virginia wound her arm around Ceana's.

"Let's go and make sure you are made welcome," she said. "And then I want you to tell me everything happening in Ireland. And Iverclaire."

Oh, dear, that would be a tale, wouldn't it?

Chapter Three

To her great surprise, her valises were taken to a guest chamber at the end of the hall on the second floor. A brass plaque on the door was inscribed with her name.

As her fingertips traced the letters, she turned to Virginia. "Have I always had my own guest room?"

Virginia smiled. "A suite. It's one thing Macrath has always insisted on. All his family is welcome at Drumvagen. Mairi has one, as does Fenella," she added, referring to the cousin who'd come to live with them as a child.

"I never knew. He is the very best brother."

"And the very best husband, except some of the time," Virginia said, smiling. She reached past Ceana to open the door.

Ever since she was a little girl, she had loved the color yellow. Macrath had evidently remembered.

The room was like a burst of sunshine when she entered. The settee was upholstered in a pale yellow with flowers embroidered on the skirt. The footstool was adorned with flowers as well, and so, too, the pale yellow carpet on the gleaming mahogany floor. Even the view of the ocean was magnificent.

"I don't know what to say," she said.

"You don't have to say a word. You're family."

Instead of leaving her, Virginia pulled her out of the room and down the corridor to the Rose Parlor, the name inscribed with another brass plaque.

The rose parlor, no doubt named for its view of Drumvagen's massive rose garden, was a thoroughly enjoyable room, one Virginia claimed as hers. This was evidenced by her very calmly locking the door so they couldn't be disturbed.

"I adore my progeny," she said, turning to Ceana. "But there are times when I need to be less their mother and more just me."

She moved to a wing chair beside the window and motioned to its companion.

"Besides, we need to talk. What has made you so upset you've come all the way from Ireland? But first, I must ask, why has Brianag declared war on you?"

She sat, watched as Virginia opened a tin of biscuits and offered it to her. Taking one, she sank her teeth into one of the most delicious chocolate biscuits she'd ever tasted.

"Do not tell me she made this," Ceana said. "I might have to reconsider how I feel about your housekeeper."

Virginia studied her for a moment, a ghost of a smile curving her lips. "Did anyone ever tell you that you sound strange? I say that as an American raised by an English nurse who's married to a Scot. I know a little about strange accents. Is it all those years living in Ireland?"

"I suspect it is."

"Brianag didn't make them," Virginia said, smiling. "They're made by a firm in Edinburgh."

Ceana reached for another biscuit. At this rate she would be waddling by the time she returned to Ireland.

She relayed the circumstances of her arrival to Virginia, including her words to Brianag. "I wasn't the least bit polite and I apologize. But she had no right to frighten Fiona. The poor child was shaking."

Virginia's face had remained very still during her recitation, but now she said, "I think it's time Brianag retired to her cottage in the village. Until recently she's always been a part of Drumvagen, but she's changed of late."

"I could be entirely wrong in my assessment," Ceana said. "Ask Fiona and Alistair. He seems to be very mature for his age."

Virginia smiled. "Logan thinks he's a born politician. One with the ability to say the most difficult things in the most pleasant way possible. Plus, he seems inordinately interested in all the news from Parliament."

Ceana's sister, Mairi, was married to Logan Harrison, the former Lord Provost of Edinburgh. The two of them had gone on to be very successful in the book publishing business. Logan also owned a very prosperous chain of bookstores, while Mairi was at the helm of the *Edinburgh Women's Gazette*, a newspaper specifically targeted to the women of Scotland.

"In a moment you'll ask about Mairi and we'll talk about Logan and then it will be time for dinner and you'll not have told me why you left Ireland."

Virginia sat back, eyeing her patiently. The time had come to tell another truth, a more personal one this time.

The course of Virginia and Macrath's love had been a

rocky one, while her own with Peter had been blessed from the very beginning. When he was taken from her, three years ago, she thought she wouldn't be able to bear it. But she had and gradually the dark night of her grief had given way to a dawn of sorts.

"I put the girls in Pegeen's care. She's my favorite sister-in-law, the one who's married to Dennis. I told her I was going to Scotland and would return in a few weeks."

"Did she ask why?" Virginia asked.

Ceana nodded. "Everyone did. I didn't know how to answer them." She took another biscuit. "The girls thought it was a grand adventure to stay with their aunt. I love my family in Ireland, truly I do. But once Peter died, everything changed. I never considered that being Peter's widow would be so much more difficult than being his wife. His family welcomed me with outstretched arms and genuinely warm hearts. Now I can't go anywhere or do anything without one of them hovering over me."

"I'll wager Peter's death was difficult for them."

She nodded. Her beloved Peter had caught a simple cold. It had lingered for a few weeks and gone into pneumonia, until his heart had simply stopped one night.

"You're their connection to Peter. If you change too much, it's like you're taking Peter away from them again."

She considered Virginia's words.

"I moved to one of the gardener's cottages on the castle grounds. You would have thought I danced naked in the light of the moon."

Virginia smiled.

She regarded the hearth, now empty of fire. In a few weeks

the room would need a full grown blaze. She might not live in Edinburgh any longer but Scottish weather didn't change.

"Is that why you're still dressed in black?"

She glanced down at herself. "I don't know if I'll ever wear anything else," she said. "Heaven knows what the brothers would do if I ever wore mauve." She glanced at Virginia. "I loved Peter with all my heart, but he's gone. I can't make him come alive, no matter how much I pray for it."

"No, you can't," Virginia said softly. "And you need a life of your own, one you choose. Have you considered moving back to Scotland?"

"I've begun to think it's the only way I can have a life," she said.

"You're always welcome at Drumvagen."

The suite she'd never before seen proved that.

When Macrath and Virginia had come to Ireland after Peter's death, the attraction between them had been difficult to witness because it reminded her too much of Peter's loss. Would it still?

Peter, too, had a way of looking at her across the room, a glance signifying love, possession, and passion. Sometimes he would smile at her, his lips barely curving, yet she would know he was vastly amused by the scene he was watching. He was a kind, considerate, thoroughly likable man, a financial genius who had taken the Duke of Lester's fortune and trebled it. Because of him, Iverclaire was positioned well for the next hundred years. Even the most profligate descendent could not hope to spend all of the money he'd amassed.

She and her daughters were also wealthy. She could easily move anywhere she wanted and not fear for lack of money.

"Thank you," she said. "Maybe that's why I came home, to see if there's a place for me here."

"You know there is." Virginia held out the tin, but this time she shook her head.

"Now tell me why this Bruce person is here at Drumvagen."

"Bruce Preston. He's a business associate of Macrath. I suspect he is investigating something to do with Macrath's newest invention. Macrath won't discuss the details with me. He told me when the time was right, he would share everything, but for now it's a secret."

How like Macrath.

She stood, walked to the window, looking down on the massive rose garden.

"Now I wish I hadn't left the girls in Ireland. They would love Drumvagen."

"Time enough for them to see it," Virginia said. "But mothers sometimes need time alone."

She nodded. Suddenly she was crying. She didn't know if she was weeping for all the confusion and misery of the last year or for the loss of Peter or for her future, unexciting as it was.

Virginia was there, a shoulder and an embrace.

That's why she was here at Drumvagen, to feel loved and to be heard.

"It was pirates," Carlton said, his bottom lip sticking out. "I saw pirates." He eyed Macrath as if calculating just how much he could push his father. "You wouldn't want me to be trapped in my room, Papa, when there were pirates about."

Any other time, Macrath might have been amused, but not now. He stood there, arms folded, staring down at his youngest son.

Virginia had almost died giving birth to Carlton. Yet he was the most adventurous and challenging of all his children. Alistair had been intelligent, curious, and perfectly mannered. Fiona was sweet, endearing, and a beauty. Carlton could never stay clean, was forever imagining things, and fought him every step of the way.

Right now he needed Carlton's obedience, which could be achieved one of two ways: punishment or cooperation.

He didn't have any doubt Carlton would get the message sooner or later, depending on the punishment he administered. He didn't want to dampen his son's enthusiasm for life, but he did want to protect him.

He came around his desk, grabbed his son by the shoulder and guided him to the chair by the fire. After moving the adjoining chair until he sat in front of the boy, he leaned forward, clasped his hands and stared straight at Carlton.

"What I'm about to tell you is to go no farther than this room, Carlton. I am not telling your brother or your sister, but I think I can trust you with the truth."

Carlton moved forward until his feet hit the floor instead of dangling in midair. He pressed his hands on the arms of the chair and nodded soberly.

"Your mother's in danger."

Carlton's eyes widened.

"It's up to all of us to protect her. I can't protect her well enough, Carlton, if I'm always worried about you doing something foolish. I need you to be a man now, not a child."

"Is it pirates?" Carlton whispered.

He shook his head. "There's a bad man who's come from America to try to steal your mother away."

"Bruce?"

He was making a mess of this, wasn't he? "No, not Bruce. Bruce is here to find the bad man."

"Does Mommy know?"

"No," he said. "Nor do I want her to know right now, Carlton. You have to stay inside Drumvagen. I will release you from your room, but I want you to stay close to your mother at all times."

Virginia wasn't going to thank him for this.

Carlton nodded enthusiastically. "I'll guard her, Papa, with my life."

Just what had his son been reading lately? He half expected Carlton to whisk out an imaginary dagger or sword. *The Count of Monte Cristo?* Did they have that in Drumvagen's library? Or had he found the old editions of the broadsides Virginia loved?

He needed to channel his son's imagination, that was obvious.

"Not forever," he said. "But for the next few weeks. I need your help, Carlton. Do you promise not to tell anyone what I've said?"

His son nodded again, less enthusiastically and more soberly this time. To his amusement, Carlton placed his hand over his heart and inclined his head in a courtier's gesture. "I do, Papa. I shall guard your secret with my life as well."

Carlton wasn't much younger than Macrath had been when his father died, leaving him to support the rest of the family. He didn't want his son aware of how cruel the world could be. Neither did he want him spoiled. A happy mix of both would be for the best.

Perhaps it wouldn't do Carlton any harm to know there was danger in the world and unfortunately it had come to Drumvagen.

CHAPTER FOUR

Bruce was a creature of habit. He chose to think of it as disciplined. Every morning, he woke at five o'clock, went running along the beach of his Massachusetts home. At least three times a week he went swimming, finding the exercise and the chill bracing. After the swim he returned to his home, eating the huge breakfast his cook had prepared.

For the rest of the day he reviewed the notes his operatives had sent him the day before. At last count he had business in four states and employed twenty men, most of them seasoned veterans of the Civil War. He preferred to work with soldiers, finding in them the same discipline he demanded of himself. Only rarely did he handle a case on his own. This one was the only recent deviation.

Macrath Sinclair had hired him ten years ago when his business was new. The other man's faith in him had kept Bruce solvent for a good many months while he tracked the man Sinclair had hired him to find.

When Paul Henderson had abruptly changed his schedule and made arrangements to travel to Scotland, Bruce telegraphed the information to Macrath and promptly followed Henderson.

Now he was sitting at a table in Drumvagen in the heart of Scotland, very far away from Massachusetts and significantly different from his daily regimen, which had been disturbed on a basic level.

On this afternoon, for example, he'd been a little homesick and took a dip in the ocean. On his return to shore he'd seen the youngest Sinclair child once again, attempting suicide by misadventure. He made it across the sand and rescued the boy, only to find himself face-to-face with yet another Sinclair, a beauty who startled him down to his toes.

Her blue eyes had singed him, stripping any words from him. He'd stood there naked, letting her look her fill. He'd never acted that way around any woman, let alone one in mourning.

"Have you been a widow long?" he now asked the woman seated opposite him.

Ceana blinked at him as if surprised. "Why would you want to know, Mr. Preston?"

He found himself smiling.

"I do apologize if I've offended you, Mrs. Mead. It was not my intent. Was your husband Irish?" There, he dared another personal question.

Her eyes narrowed.

Macrath was smiling faintly, while his wife was looking from Ceana to him as if fascinated by their byplay.

"Yes," Ceana said.

He suspected that was the only response he was going to get.

"How did you meet?" he asked.

Her lips thinned. Was she going to lose her temper? What would Ceana Mead be like angry?

She absolutely fascinated him, and he didn't have time to be fascinated by anyone, let alone an Irish widow. Correction, a Scottish widow with an Irish sounding voice.

"Macrath took Ceana to London for a season," Virginia said.

He glanced at his hostess. She had a beautiful smile, and he'd seen it often in the two weeks he'd been here.

"Ceana and I became friends," Virginia continued. "I always looked for her at the events I attended."

"And I couldn't help but notice the beautiful American," Macrath added.

"You're an American?" he asked Virginia, genuinely surprised.

"From upstate New York," she said, naming a town with which he was quite familiar. "My father was Harold Anderson."

Harold Anderson had been a tycoon in every sense of the word. At one time, the man had his hand in everything.

Bruce sat back, surprised. "Yet here you are, in the middle of Scotland."

"Yes," she said smiling again. "Aren't I blessed?"

He had the feeling Macrath was the one who was truly blessed.

"Is that where you met your husband, Mrs. Mead?" he asked, turning to Ceana. "In London?"

She stared at him. He was pretty good at reading people and he could swear there was a glimmer of annoyance in Ceana's eyes.

"Yes," she said. "Are you married, Mr. Preston?"

Instead of answering her, he asked, "Do you like to swim, Mrs. Mead?"

To his amusement, her cheeks turned pink. Was she recalling the sight of him naked?

"Only when there is no one around, Mr. Preston," she said. "If someone might spy on me, for example, I am modest to a fault. More than I can say for a great many people."

Macrath laughed. "Are you calling me immodest, Ceana?" He glanced at his wife. "No more cuddling on the beach for us, my love."

Ceana lifted her eyes to the ceiling, prompting Bruce's further amusement.

He concentrated on his plate for a few minutes. "I must congratulate you on your cook," he said to Macrath. "The meal is easily the equal of anything I've had in New York City."

He was on his best behavior for the rest of dinner, which meant he ignored Ceana. From time to time he would glance in her direction then look away when she noticed.

He'd never seen a woman so beautiful in black. She was the epitome of suffering, and he'd seen his share. He still recalled every memory of the war, of the carnage he'd seen and the widows and orphans he'd had to greet. He had found something good to say about every man in his command. They'd all been soldiers, most of them unwilling and unprepared to go to war, but they'd done so anyway. More than a few had died with surprise on their faces.

He wanted to know her story. Who was her husband? How had he died? Where had she lived? Why, of all of them at the dinner table, did he seek out her smile the most?

Perhaps it had something to do with the look she'd given him earlier. He could have mistaken the hunger on her expression. He could have simply wanted to see it.

When they moved away from the dinner table and into the small parlor, Macrath and Virginia addressed them both.

"I hope you'll forgive our absence for a few minutes," Macrath said. "It's time to tuck our brood into bed."

And check on Carlton, if he didn't miss his guess.

He went to stand beside the fireplace, resting one hand on the mantel just inches away from the frame of the family portrait. It was of Macrath, Virginia, and their three children. On the opposite wall there was another member of the family with the Sinclair eyes. On a third wall there was a picture of Ceana along with a redheaded man. She was younger there but her eyes still sparkled as they had in the grotto. Her husband's expression was one of adoration, and her smile was ripe with joy.

Even a blind man could see she'd been in love.

"Did you still love him on the day he died?" he asked, turning to her. She gave him a blank look at first, and then her expression melted into anger.

"What kind of question is that to ask, Mr. Preston?"

"An intrusive one," he said. "An impertinent one. Possibly even a rude one."

She looked surprised at his self-indictment.

"Yet I can't help but want to know. If you loved him on the day he died, he died a happy man. Not all men can say as much, Mrs. Mead."

She turned her head and studied the portrait she'd studiously avoided until now.

"I loved him with my whole heart," she said.

"Then I envy the man, dead as he is."

She shook her head at him. "You have to stop saying things like that."

"Most people think it's because I'm an American. We're a little crass sometimes."

"Nonsense. I've known my share of Americans, including Virginia. They were all extraordinarily polite people. All but you, Mr. Preston."

She grabbed the material on the backside of her dress, moved it so she could sit.

"Why do women insist on having a bustle over their bottom?" he asked. "Do you have no idea how ridiculous you look?"

Her eyes were blazing at him now, her cheeks pink. He hid his smile with difficulty.

"Are you an expert at fashion? Or do you think it would be better for me to appear naked at dinner?"

"I doubt I should have finished my meal in that case, Mrs. Mead."

She had the most enchanting expression on her face, a combination of surprise and irritation.

"Where do you live?"

"None of your concern," she said.

"Why have you come to Drumvagen?"

"Again, none of your concern."

"How long will you be staying?"

She folded her hands, straightened her shoulders and smiled thinly up at him. "Do sit down, Mr. Preston. If you're going to continue with your marathon of questions, shouldn't you at least be comfortable? Or must you overpower everyone with your size?"

"Who's being crass now, Mrs. Mead? Is it entirely polite for a woman to comment on a man's . . . size?"

Her entire face was flushed, but her eyes sparkled merrily at him. He was certain Ceana was enjoying their encounter.

"Never mind," he said, taking the chair opposite the settee. He made no pretense of looking away, but studied her intently. "I can find out the answer to most of those questions."

"Why would you even care?"

He settled back, resting his ankle on his knee and placing his hands on the arms of the chair.

"Because you fascinate me. I'm curious about a great many things, Mrs. Mead. Such as you. I find myself wanting to know all manner of things about you."

She looked away, presenting him a perfect profile. She had a stubborn chin, an aquiline nose, and lips that interested him entirely too much.

How did she kiss? Did she throw herself wholeheartedly into passion or did she need to be coaxed into it?

"You never answered me," he said. "How long has it been since your husband died?"

She turned to look at him, and to his shock there were tears in her eyes. He stood and before she could say a scathing word to him was beside her on the settee, pulling out his handkerchief and pressing it into her hand.

"Oh for the love of God, Ceana, I didn't mean to make you cry."

She smiled and the expression of tears and humor made his heart turn over in his chest.

"You didn't," she said. "Oh, very well, maybe you did. Everyone has been so careful not to talk about my husband, as if doing so might resurrect him. As if Peter would appear like a ghost in the middle of the parlor. Peter would never haunt anyone. He was always so careful to consider everyone's opinion and wishes."

The man sounded like one of those diffident creatures he'd encountered occasionally who were so anxious to please other people they never pleased themselves.

"I really can be extraordinarily rude at times," he said. "Forgive me."

She pressed his handkerchief to her cheeks, mopping up her tears.

If Macrath Sinclair entered the room now he would think that his sister had been abused in some fashion.

"Why are you here?" she asked, surprising him. "What secret do you and Macrath share? Is it a new invention? Why won't he talk about it?"

He stared at her.

"You see how annoying it is, Mr. Preston?"

He began to smile.

"Are you married, Mr. Preston?"

"Not anymore," he said.

"That means you once were. I'm sorry."

"It was a very long time ago, Mrs. Mead. I do not pull on the scab of my grief in order to feel it every day."

"Is that what you think I'm doing?" she asked.

"Only you can answer that question."

"If you must know, Mr. Preston, I was not crying for my husband. I was missing my daughters. Do you have children?"

"Not anymore," he said, standing.

She'd turned the tables on him quite ably, hadn't she?

He left before she could ask him anything else.

CHAPTER FIVE

"Aunt Ceana?" Fiona said, standing in the doorway of the Tartan Parlor. "May I ask you a question?"

"Of course you can," Ceana said, making room on the settee for Fiona.

Her niece sat beside her, folded her hands very primly and looked at her somberly.

"Is it so terrible living in Ireland? Do you miss Scotland so very much? Papa said you must. I couldn't imagine living anywhere else but at Drumvagen. But I suppose I must, because one day I'll marry and move away."

"And you're afraid you might go as far away as Ireland, is that it?"

Fiona nodded.

"I doubt you will," Ceana said. "But if you fall in love and wish to marry someone, the distance won't matter. You'll go anywhere with him and hardly notice where you are."

"Does it hurt very much to be in love?"

What a question. How on earth did she answer? Perhaps

it would be better to direct the girl to her mother, but then Fiona continued.

"Sometimes I see them, my parents, and they look at each other and there is such pain in their eyes."

Oh dear.

"I don't think it's pain at all, Fiona. I think it's love you're seeing. I was there, at the very beginning, you see. I remember when they first saw each other and it was like no other person existed for Virginia and Macrath. Or nobody was ever more important to my brother and your mother."

Fiona threaded her fingers together.

"Sometimes I think they don't notice when anyone else is in the room."

"That's a wonderful thing, don't you think? A mother and a father should love each other the most first and then their children. Your grandfather, for example, spoke fondly of your grandmother every day of his life. When he died, it was with her name on his lips. I like to think he saw her at that moment and went to join her in heaven."

"Like you'll go and join Uncle Peter?"

The child knew how to ask questions, didn't she?

Very well, she would turn the tables on her. "How do you like being the only girl in the household?"

Fiona sighed. "I do wish I had a sister. But then, she'd probably steal my hairbrush and want to wear my ribbons. Carlton steals things from me all the time, but he never wishes to wear my clothes."

Ceana bit back her laughter with difficulty.

"There's always a first time," Bruce said.

She looked up to find the man grinning at her.

"I wouldn't put it past Carlton to wear your clothes and pretend to be you, Fiona, in order to escape Drumvagen. He's the master of escape."

Fiona nodded. "He would. He doesn't like to be confined. Or punished." She sighed. "He's very trying for a younger brother."

"I can attest it's also very trying to be the youngest," Ceana said.

"Did you disobey your father?" Fiona asked.

"Indeed I did not."

"Or tell tales that couldn't possibly be true?"

She really couldn't lie to her niece. "Maybe once or twice."

"I would wager you didn't stow aboard ship because you wanted to see America," Bruce said.

"Oh, dear, did he really do that?" Her nephew sounded a great deal more adventurous than any of the family.

She heard Virginia calling her daughter. Before she could alert Fiona to her mother's summons, the girl had scooted off the settee and was at the door.

"Thank you, Aunt Ceana," she said, and smiled in parting, a gamine expression equally distributed between Ceana and Bruce.

She smiled after her niece. Her daughters would like Fiona. She truly needed to bring them home. They would love Scotland.

Bruce stared out the window at the waves rolling into shore. What was he thinking? That she wanted to know was a surprise.

"Why are you here, Mr. Preston?"

He turned his head and studied her.

"I'm not at liberty to discuss it with you, Mrs. Mead. I would if I could."

He was the most annoying man.

"Tell me about your children," he said.

She eyed him. "To what purpose?"

His smile was wry, as if he mocked his interest or her protectiveness.

"Can't I simply be interested?" he asked, coming to sit beside her.

She wasn't certain it was wise for him to be interested or for her to feel pleased. She looked out at the view, feeling like she was on a tiny island surrounded by the ocean. All she could see was Kinloch Bay and beyond to the North Sea.

"I have two daughters," she said. "Ten and seven. Nessa is the youngest and the mischievous one. Darina's more solemn. She worries about everything, and that worries me."

"Were you the same?"

She considered the question.

"I don't think I was. I was the youngest. First, there was Mairi, then Macrath, then me. Even after our father died and I knew we didn't have much money, I didn't worry. I knew Macrath would take care of me. Or Mairi."

"You were fortunate to have such protectors."

She nodded.

She hadn't forgotten his response when she asked if he had children. He said "not anymore," leaving her filled with curiosity. But it wasn't a question she could easily ask. Instead, she let silence envelop them.

The sea breeze from the open window cooled the room, brought the scent of the ocean inside.

He didn't talk or try to fill the silence with platitudes. Instead, he sat beside her as quiet as she, seemingly content.

She put her hand on the settee. Her little finger was only a short distance from his hand. They were so close yet so far away.

"My wife was from Mississippi," he said. "We met during the graduation ceremony at West Point. Her brother was a good friend of mine."

She didn't turn, didn't look at him, merely inspected the toes of her shoes peeping out from beneath her skirt.

"I knew about the tension between the states, but I never expected the situation to escalate to war. She'd taken the children to visit their grandparents in Mississippi. The day Fort Sumter was fired on, I was given my own division. Suddenly, the South was my enemy and my in-laws were traitors."

He didn't say anything else for a few moments. He simply sat studying the tartan pattern of the settee.

"She was stuck behind enemy lines." He turned his head to look at her. "That's how I was told to think of it. It took me a year to get to Mississippi."

She really didn't want to hear anymore. She wanted to wave her hand and send him from the room, allow her to think about her own children safe at Iverclaire.

Most of all she wanted to banish the spike of fear deep inside warning her of the horror of his tale. But once curiosity had been set free, it was difficult to quash it entirely. The question of his wife and children's fate hung in her mind, desperate to be answered.

"Daniel was five. Sarah was six."

"You never saw them again?"

"No."

The one word was too simple, filled with such hopelessness she wanted to weep.

"After the war I tried once more. This time I found my sister-in-law."

When he finally spoke again, she let out a relieved sigh, then caught her breath in the next second.

"She led me to all three graves," he said, lowering his head to study his interlinked hands. "I don't know what was worse, knowing or not knowing."

"How did they die?" she softly asked.

"Corinth was a hospital town," he said. "Soldiers returning from Shiloh were sent there, but the town wasn't prepared for hundreds of thousands of men. People died of the heat, of dysentery, of other diseases. So did my family."

He looked away. "It was a very long time ago."

"Do you ever truly forget such things? Is there enough time in the world to cope with such loss?"

He stood, glancing down at her, his fascinating eyes gleaming. "Perhaps not. But sooner or later you have to make a choice. To live in the world as it is. Or to sit wishing and hoping things were different. Wishing and hoping never made anything change."

Before she could say anything else, he left her sitting there, staring after him, feeling as if she'd failed in some elemental and important way.

He hadn't intended to tell her anything. He never talked about his wife or children. Instead, they were locked away in a vault in his mind.

Then why had he?

There was something about Ceana Mead that called to him. Maybe it was her nurturing nature? After all, she was trying to save Carlton when he first saw her. Fiona had taken to her immediately and Alistair couldn't say enough good things about her. Or maybe it was the way she had of looking at him that seemed to burrow down into the core of him where the real Bruce lay, the person he never showed anyone.

He hadn't wanted her pity, but perhaps he craved her understanding.

She had a directness about her that he hadn't found in many women. But then he wasn't in the company of women much. Had that been a conscious decision? If so, here at Drumvagen he had no option but to notice Ceana.

He wondered about her marriage. She said she'd loved Peter with all her heart. Did she miss the man the way he'd once missed Kate, as if part of his life had been turned to ashes at her death?

In the beginning he'd had to make a choice each day, the same one he suspected Ceana was making now. To live or to will himself to die. To choose to put one foot in front of the other, to enjoy life without guilt, to accumulate a treasure trove of memories having nothing to do with Kate or his children. To begin to build a life alone.

Was she doing that? And why did he care so much?

CHAPTER SIX

"I recommend you tell her, Macrath. It's the only way we can make sure she's safe."

"I don't want her to know. I just thank God Ceana is here now. Virginia won't notice the extra precautions I'm taking."

"The more she's aware, the better."

Ceana halted outside Macrath's library.

What were they discussing? Something they evidently didn't want Virginia to know.

She was instantly annoyed on her sister-in-law's behalf. Such behavior reminded her of her brothers-in-law. They, too, were set on proscribing behavior—hers—and ensuring any choice was taken from her.

Her brother was the most obstinate person she'd ever known, which turned out to be great training for handling three Irish brothers-in-law. Now she wanted to enter his library and demand he tell Virginia whatever it was he was trying to hide.

His next words kept her silent and in place.

"I can't abide the idea of Virginia being frightened."

What on earth was he talking about?

They shouldn't have left the door ajar. Nor should she have such a curious nature. She really should leave, pretend she hadn't heard anything and go to the gazebo, her original destination this morning.

How was she supposed to un-hear what she had heard?

"You know your wife better than I, Macrath, but Virginia doesn't strike me as the type of person to be frightened by a threat. Instead, I would imagine she would go after him herself."

Macrath laughed. "You might be right. Still, it's my duty to protect her. And I don't want her knowing."

"I'll accede to your wishes, but I think knowing about the threat, your wife would be better equipped to handle it."

"On this we're just going to have to disagree."

From the sound of Macrath's voice, he was moving closer to the door. She scuttled backward, entered the hallway and made her way out the back of Drumvagen.

The passage of years hadn't softened her brother's obstinacy. If she went to Macrath and ask, he'd simply refuse to tell her. Nor could she, in all good conscience, go to Virginia and tell her what she'd overheard. Doing so would be in direct violation of Macrath's wishes.

No, she needed to get Mr. Preston alone and find out what was going on at Drumvagen.

Bruce had been warned about Scottish weather, but so far he hadn't found it appreciably different from his Massachusetts home. Scottish winters couldn't be any more deadly than one accompanied by a frigid wind off the Atlantic. Still, he hoped to be home by the time of the first snow, a thought that would have pleased him a week ago. When had it changed?

He stopped on the path, surprise keeping him still. Ceana was sitting in the gazebo, her attention on something he couldn't see. He could circumvent the structure and continue on to the village or make his presence known.

Since she'd been on his mind since the night before, he veered off the path and headed for the gazebo.

He stood at the steps, his hands on either side of the columns.

"Since I've told you about my wife, it's only fair you tell me about your husband."

"Is it?"

She'd been gazing at a letter. She looked up, regarding him somberly, her deep blue eyes mysterious and captivating.

"I apologize. I didn't mean to interrupt you. I'll leave you to your letter."

"I have no intention of reading it," she said, holding the envelope up for him to see. "It's from Ireland. No doubt one of my brothers-in-law fussing at me. I didn't get permission before I left, you see."

"Why did you need permission?"

She sighed. "I'm my husband's widow." She looked off into the distance. "Peter's been dead for three years," she said. "Most people normally don't mention him, as if doing so erases my grief. Was it the same for you?"

"Yes. You loved him very much."

"Yes. And your wife?"

"The same. How did he die?"

"A cold," she said. "Just a cold. He must have been feeling very bad but he never said anything to anyone. One night he went to sleep and simply didn't wake up. The physician said it was pneumonia involving his heart."

"And so you came to Scotland."

A smile trembled on her lips. "And so I came to Scotland. Not to escape my grief, Mr. Preston, but my in-laws, all of whom think I should have been buried with my husband."

"You're jesting," he said, taking a seat to her right.

"According to my brothers-in-law, I should remain a proper widow for the rest of my days."

"They're damn idiots if they think that," he said.

Her eyes widened at his profanity.

"I apologize, but I can't imagine a worse fate. What are you, in your twenties? You've got a long life ahead of you. Are you supposed to be dead because your husband died?"

"I'm a little older," she said, "but I thank you for the compliment, Mr. Preston."

"Bruce," he said. "My name is Bruce. You must call me that, otherwise I can't call you Ceana. It would be an inconvenience for me to have to translate your name to Mrs. Mead before I speak."

"You are the most surprising man," she said.

"Why? Because I say what I think?"

"Is that entirely wise, saying what you think?"

"Decidedly not," he said, staring at her mouth. "Otherwise, I wouldn't tell you I've wanted to kiss you from the moment I saw you, widow or not."

Her fingers pressed against her mouth as if to banish any improvident comment or hide her lips from him. The first she might be able to do, but never the second. He would kiss her ear, then maybe behind it, down her neck and up again. He'd make her gasp and lose control of herself and then he'd have that lush mouth of hers.

A week, that's how long it had been since he lost his reason. From the very first moment he saw Ceana Sinclair Mead.

She had to leave.

He was making her think things she had no business thinking. Very well, perhaps he wasn't actually *making* her think those things, but he shouldn't say things like that to her. He shouldn't make her pulse race in such a manner.

His eyes were so attractive, reminding her of a tumbler of the best Scottish whiskey with light shooting through it.

His chin was square, his throat strong, his shoulders almost too large for the white shirt he wore. She had absolutely no intention of allowing her eyes to stray below his waist in memory of what he looked like naked.

She was not a woman to engage in fantasies, and he was very much a fantasy.

"What must Virginia not know?" she asked, gratified to see his face change. The teasing grin was instantly gone and in its place were thinned lips and a flat stare.

"I don't know what you're talking about," he said.

"Nonsense, of course you do. You and Macrath were discussing something in his library. He didn't want to tell Virginia something and you were all set for letting her know. What was it?"

"You misheard, I'm afraid."

She sat back against the gazebo bench and folded her arms, giving him a parental stare, one capable of freezing her daughters in place.

"You're lying. I'm very good at ferreting out liars, and you're lying."

"You're mistaken."

"Very well, then I'll just go to Virginia and tell her what I overheard. She'll get it out of Macrath sooner or later."

He actually had the effrontery to grin at her.

He had been so much more receptive to her tears. What a pity she wasn't the type to weep on command.

"You really must tell me," she said.

"I must?"

She nodded. "It's the gentlemanly thing to do."

"I regret I will have to be ungentlemanly, then."

"She's my dear friend and my sister-in-law. If she's in danger, I should know."

"You don't trust Macrath to protect her?"

She sighed. "Of course I do."

"Then leave it, Ceana."

"How can I?"

He looked away, staring through the trees.

"What do you know about Paul Henderson?" he finally asked.

She shook her head. "I've never heard the name."

"He was employed by her first husband in London. As a caregiver."

She nodded. "I remember. Lawrence was an invalid."

"From what I understand, Henderson developed an attraction to Virginia. He kidnapped her."

She hadn't heard that story.

"What happened?"

"Henderson was all set to take her to America, but Virginia escaped."

"And so did Paul," she said, guessing. "Which is why you're here."

He nodded. "Macrath hired me a decade ago to find Henderson."

"And you did," she guessed. "Have you been watching him all this time?"

"When I realized he was on his way back to Britain, I informed Macrath."

She remained quiet, hoping he would tell her the rest of the story. To her relief, he continued.

"I followed him to Scotland, but lost him outside of Inverness. I don't doubt, however, he's on his way here."

"Surely he doesn't have a fixation on Virginia after all these years?"

"One man's obsession might be considered another man's love."

"But surely he understands how much she loves Macrath?" A thought occurred to her. "You don't think Virginia's in danger. You think Macrath's the one he's after."

He shrugged. "At this point it doesn't matter which one. I'd just as soon rid the world of Paul Henderson." At her look, he smiled. "No, I don't mean killing the man. But in America we couldn't prosecute him for a kidnapping taking place on Scottish soil."

"But once he came back to Scotland he could be arrested," she finished.

He nodded again.

"Now you have to find him before he hurts Macrath or Virginia."

"I do."

"I agree with Macrath," she said. "It wouldn't do to tell Virginia."

He studied her. "Why?"

"Virginia worries, and I don't mean about her safety, but about Macrath. My brother can sometimes be rash and imprudent."

"I find him to be measured and deliberate."

"Then you don't know Macrath as well as you think. He loves Virginia. When you love someone, you aren't always measured and deliberate."

"Is that how it was with you?"

The gazebo was suddenly too warm and he too close, even though he was on the other side of the structure.

"There are many types of love, Mr. Preston."

"So it wasn't."

"I adored my husband."

She sat there regarding him, trying to rein in her temper. He was everything she didn't like in a man: arrogant, condescending, self-righteous, too confident. Plus, there was a look in his eyes that made a flush travel from her heels all the way up to linger on her cheeks.

Someone should tell him it wasn't proper to look at a widow the way he was looking at her. Someone should tell him he should keep a proper expression on his face, not allow his lips to turn up on one corner as if he found the situation amusing.

Someone should also tell him she was not the kind of woman who flirted with a man she barely knew, even if the man had appeared stark naked in front of her.

He had quite a nice backside, and why on earth was she remembering that now?

"People tell you you're right most of the time, don't they? I'm surprised they don't bow in front of you. Do the women all giggle and scamper about?"

He only continued to smile at her, as if her words didn't discomfit him one bit. Or as if he knew how agitated she was, although she was certain she didn't reveal it in any way.

"Go away, Mr. Preston. Bruce. Whichever name you prefer. Go away, leaving me to my contemplation of nature."

"You want to be alone?" he asked.

"Yes, I most fervently do," she said, turning and focusing her attention on a venerable oak.

One moment he was sitting across the way and the next standing in front of her, hauling her up into his arms and placing his mouth on hers.

Her lips fell open in surprise as he laid claim to her mouth. She told her arms to remain at her side. Ordered her back to stiffen. But, oh, her treacherous arms wound around his neck, and when he took a step forward, she bent backward like a sapling in a gale.

He was kissing her and she was letting him. Worse, she was participating. Her heart was furiously beating, her breath coming so fast she wondered if she'd tightened her corset too much this morning.

She was burning up. It was not yet noon yet she was desperately overheated. The sun wasn't doing that to her. This annoying, arrogant man was kissing her into a fever.

Desire spread through her body. Joy, anticipation, the sheer delight of being alive made her tremble.

What was she doing?

She was allowing a perfect stranger to kiss her. Worse, if he pushed the issue, she might well succumb on the floor of the gazebo.

With the last of her reason she pulled back. She placed one hand against his chest, feeling his heart beating as fast as hers. Head bowed, she prayed for some type of restraint as well as the ability to speak.

"Virginia would be miserable worrying about Macrath."

"Love does that," he said. "They love each other very much."

She nodded. Should he be talking about love to her? Especially when they stood so close and she still tasted him on her lips.

She pressed her hand against his chest, feeling like he was a wall of brick or stone, something impenetrable and immobile. He must release her. He must step back and remove temptation from her.

As if he heard her words, he took two steps back, dropping his arms. He didn't, however, apologize. Nor would she be such a hypocrite to demand it. She hadn't been a victim but a willing participant.

She took a step to the left, then another, making here way to the entrance of the gazebo. Only then did she turn and look at him directly.

"You will be careful, won't you?"

"I'm normally careful," he said. "Normally."

She was being silly, imagining words that hadn't been said. But as she left the gazebo, careful not to look back, she could have sworn he said, "Except when it comes to you."

CHAPTER SEVEN

She placed herself in exile for the next two days, taking her meals on a tray in the lovely sitting room that was part of her suite.

When Virginia came to see her after breakfast the first morning, she had no other choice but to assure her sister-in-law she was fine, just a little tired from the journey.

"It's nothing else, Ceana? Is it the children? Have they been a bother?"

"They could never be a bother. They're all wonderful and you know it."

"Macrath? Has he said something to upset you?"

She smiled. "No. He's been Macrath and that's never upsetting." She smiled at her sister-in-law. "Truly, it's nothing. I thought being lazy for a day or two might be for the best."

Virginia was finally assured of her health and her mood. She didn't need to know about her confusion or the fact she was perilously close to tears most of the time.

She missed her girls and she missed Peter, but above all she missed herself.

Her brothers-in-law would have her remain in black, becoming the matriarch of the family. She would be spoken about in whispers. *Dear Aunt Ceana, widowed all these years. She never quite survived the death of her beloved husband. Shush, don't speak so loud. You are in the company of our straight-laced Aunt Ceana. She is the bulwark of the family, the morality expert. She dictates and passes judgments on others.*

Oh, but she didn't want to be like Brianag.

She wanted to live. Dear God, she wanted to feel delight and joy and happiness once again. She wanted to rear her daughters to be strong women. She wanted to show them life was a series of events, some good, some bad, but they could weather them all.

How did she do that if she retreated into darkness? If she became the black cloud over Iverclaire?

She wanted passion, and if that single wish and desire tainted her soul, then so be it. She could not forget she was alive. After Bruce's kiss, how could she? That spike of desire she'd felt had shocked her.

Perhaps she locked herself in her suite as punishment. Or to hide from temptation.

Oh, he was a temptation wasn't he? With his grin and his surprising eyes and his deep and masculine voice. He'd incited her compassion and her tears, yet now all she could think about was how he kissed.

Would he be a good lover?

No one had ever told her, prior to her marriage, she might enjoy the physical aspects of love so much. When Peter was taken from her, that was gone as well. Was she so terrible for wanting to feel desire again? Was she a harlot?

She needed to see a man of God. Peter's family was Presbyterian, like she'd been reared, but sometimes she wished they were Catholic. How nice it must be to go see a priest and confess all her sins and be given penance for them. As it was, she was the only one to dole out her punishment: being a hermit in her rooms.

Bruce Preston was still too much on her mind, however.

On the morning of the third day, she left her suite, slipped down the back stairs, and escaped Drumvagen almost miraculously. Brianag didn't stop her in the corridor. None of the children saw her. Her only witness was a young maid who smiled brightly as she carried a bucket of cleaning supplies up the stairs.

She knew, from conversations among the children, there were at least three ways to the village of Kinloch. She took the easiest way, the road leading from the back of the house, hugging the cliffs.

It was bright, no clouds overhead to mar the promise of a beautiful day. Seabirds called to her as she walked. The incoming tide whispering over the sand sounded like her name: Ceana.

How many people worked at Drumvagen? In addition to the barn and the stables some distance from the house, there were the buildings housing Macrath's refrigeration machines. She counted five of those, each one closer to the village than the next. Did he own all the land between Drumvagen and Kinloch?

A surge of pride made her smile. Macrath had achieved everything he'd wanted as a boy in Edinburgh. Nor had he been stingy with his good fortune. Look how intent he'd been to ensure she had a chance at a bright future, too. If he hadn't paid for and accompanied her during her London season, she would never have met Peter. Macrath, in turn, would never have met Virginia.

Fate had a large hand in their romantic destinies.

"You shouldn't be on the road alone."

She jerked, startled and turned to face Bruce.

"I'm only going to Kinloch," she said. "No farther."

"Nevertheless, you shouldn't be alone."

"This Henderson person doesn't want me. I doubt if he even knows I exist."

"I'm not willing to take that chance," he said. "I don't want any harm to come to you." He reached out his hand, the backs of his fingers brushing her cheek.

She took a step back. "I have to go to the village."

"Then fine, I'll accompany you."

"That wouldn't be acceptable. I'm going to see the minister. I've been told that Kinloch has a lovely church."

"Are you feeling the need of spiritual guidance?"

She only shook her head.

"You're going to go ask him if it's all right if you continue living."

How did he know that?

"Go back to Drumvagen, Bruce," she said, beginning to walk again.

"Are you going to ask for expiation for that, too? For calling me Bruce as opposed to Mr. Preston? How improper you can be, Ceana."

She stopped in the middle of the road, folded her arms and glared at him.

"Are you going to follow me all the way to Kinloch?"

"Yes. I have your safety to consider as well as the rest of the family. Besides, I can give you as much spiritual guidance as your minister."

She ignored him and continued walking.

"You may call me Reverend Preston."

"Don't be sacrilegious."

His grin was too captivating. She simply couldn't look in his direction.

"I would say to you, Ceana Mead, there's nothing wrong with wanting to live, even after such a disastrous loss."

He was speaking from personal experience, which made it difficult to discount his words.

"I'm living," she said.

"You're breathing and you're moving, but are you really living?"

She stopped again.

"Who are you to judge me?"

"The man who kissed you."

She stared at him wide eyed.

"Has no other man kissed you but Peter?"

Surely she wasn't supposed to answer that?

He moved closer to her. Even though they were standing in the middle of a paved road, it seemed too intimate. She wanted to put her hand on his chest and push him away. No, she mustn't touch him.

"It took years for me to realize that short of doing myself in, I was going to live. I would spare you some of that wasted time."

"Did you never think of doing yourself in?" The idea had never occurred to her because of her daughters. But for him, the situation was different. He had lost his children in addition to his wife.

"No," he said. "There was a time when I tried to kill myself with whiskey, but I began to loathe the taste of it, not to mention what it made me feel like in the morning."

She turned and began to walk again, but slower now.

"If I take a case of someone who needs protection," Bruce said, "I'll do everything in my power to ensure they're safe."

"There's no need for kisses, though," she said, not looking at him.

"Oh, no, that was just for me."

He showed no signs of dropping back. Would he walk all the way to Kinloch with her, sit outside the church while she spoke to the minister? What on earth would she say?

There's this man who troubles me, Reverend. He's too handsome for my peace of mind. When he grins at me I lose my train of thought. When he kissed me, I almost fainted with desire.

That wouldn't do, would it?

She stole a glance at him. He was smiling at her.

Against such an implacable will, what choice did she have?

She shook her head, turned on her heel and began walking back to the house.

"Very well," she said. "I'll go back to Drumvagen and be a hermit there. But I have to return to Ireland soon. You can't think of stopping me."

"I only ask that you not leave until we find Henderson. I can't guarantee your safety otherwise."

"Then do hurry up and find the idiotic man," she said.

Did he realize that he was one of the reasons why she was thinking of leaving so soon?

They walked together. To her surprise, he didn't feel the need to fill the silence with words.

"Tell me about your home," she said a few minutes later.

"I have a house near Boston," he said. "It's close enough to the city that I don't feel isolated, but it sits on a bluff overlooking the ocean."

"Have you always lived there?"

Did he realize what she was asking? From his smile, it seemed as if he did.

"Only for the last five years," he said.

So there weren't memories in every room, around every corner, unlike her situation in Ireland.

Iverclaire was a grand castle, more than adequate for the four brothers and their wives, with room left over for a dozen more family members.

She'd found refuge from memories by moving into one of the abandoned gardener's cottages on the estate. It boasted three rooms, adequate space for her and the girls. The kitchen was ample, opening up into a large sitting room. The girls had one bedroom and she the other. More than anything else, it offered privacy and silence, blessed silence.

"Macrath and I grew up in Edinburgh, and I'm surprised he chose to live here."

"While I greet the Atlantic each day. The ocean appears angry most of the time, unlike here."

"My daughters would like the beach," she said. "And the grotto."

She felt her cheeks warm at the mention of the grotto and wished she hadn't said anything. He would think she was recalling the first time she saw him, and of course she was doing no such thing. That the image of him on the beach was seared into her mind was something she needed to remedy.

At the base of the back stairs she turned to face him.

He held out his hand and she placed hers in it.

"I want you safe, Ceana."

By his words he meant for her to stay close to Drumvagen. Did he also mean to avoid him? She had a feeling she should do both.

She nodded, pulled her hand free and began to mount the steps, forcing herself not to look back at him.

CHAPTER EIGHT

"I'm really worried about her," Virginia said, slipping into bed beside her husband.

Macrath gathered her up in his arms and addressed the ceiling. "We have a plethora of females in our household, so you could mean any one of them. Fiona? One of the maids? Brianag?"

She slapped his chest. "You know I mean Ceana. She isn't herself."

"At least she's not hiding in her room."

She raised up and stared at him in the darkness, wishing she hadn't extinguished the lamp.

"She was fatigued."

"She was malingering," he said. "Ceana often retreats when she doesn't know how to handle a situation or she's avoiding it."

"What situation is she avoiding?" she asked, dropping back onto the mattress.

"I'm not sure. Maybe the decision to move home. Maybe Bruce."

"Bruce?"

He chuckled and tightened his arm around her. "Haven't you seen the looks they give each other? Part animosity, part interest. They're just like Mairi and Logan were. Bruce couldn't stop looking at Ceana and she studiously avoided looking anywhere in his direction."

She had noticed, but thought Ceana didn't like the American. A pity, since she truly liked Bruce Preston. So did Macrath.

"I think we should invite Marie and Logan here. And Finella as well."

"A reunion would be nice," she said.

He shook his head. "No, not simply a reunion Perhaps all of us can convince her to remain in Scotland."

"I don't think there's any problem with that," Virginia said. "Ceana needs a place to stay. Granted, she can go and live in Edinburgh, but wouldn't it be lovely to have her here? I have missed her so."

"You think she would move to Drumvagen?"

"I do, but the decision must be hers."

She wouldn't pressure Ceana, unlike her Irish relatives.

Cuddling closer to her husband, she was thankful, in this relationship at least, there was no confusion as to emotions. She adored Macrath and knew he felt the same about her.

Wouldn't it be wonderful if Ceana would fall in love again? Once, she herself had felt the same way, never thinking love would come to her again. She'd needed a certain measure of fearlessness, a courage she'd never thought to possess, but she'd won Macrath in the end.

The question was: did Ceana want to fall in love? Or was her heart buried with Peter?

Ceana stood at the window of her sitting room, staring out over black moonless sky. From here you couldn't tell there was an ocean only a short distance away. The darkness, the blackness, was absolute.

Not unlike her life these past three years.

She wanted to be kissed again. She wanted to be loved. Without thinking, without passing judgment, without even allowing herself to wonder about what she was doing, she opened her door and stood there, listening to the sounds of night at Drumvagen.

The wind whistled around the house but there were no drafts in the corridor. Macrath had built a solid home for his clan. A dozen feet away was the door to another guest suite. A dozen feet, that's all.

She held the wrapper tight against her body, turned and closed her door, then measured the steps she took down the corridor. The faint light from the wall sconce at the end of the hall illuminated the carving on the door as well as the brass handle.

Softly, she rapped on the door, giving herself a test. If he didn't answer at the faint sound, she would turn, retreat to her room, and counsel herself against any further foolishness.

The door opened so suddenly she wondered if he'd been waiting for her.

He didn't say a word, merely extended his hand, palm up. She swallowed, placed her hand atop his and allowed him to draw her inside. He reached behind her to close the door, the latch a snick of sound in the silence.

He didn't say a word, either welcoming or condemning, only drew her farther into the sitting room. The lit lamp on the table beside the settee was the only illumination, but it seemed as bright as a summer sun.

In the middle of the room, he faced her.

He was still dressed in a white shirt and black trousers, but her mind held the picture of what he'd looked like naked. Unless he sent her away or her own conscience banished her from the room, she would see him naked again.

She'd be able to touch him.

Her hands were at her sides, her wrapper held fast by a single button at her neck. Her nightwear was black as well, her mourning attire complete. Even at night she was not supposed to forget she was a widow.

He bent his head, his attention focused on the single button. When it was undone, he slipped the garment off her shoulders, letting it fall to the floor.

"I've never known any woman as beautiful in black as you, Ceana."

She closed her eyes.

Don't let him question me. Don't let him ask me why I'm here. Don't let him make me say the words.

He bent his head, placed an almost chaste kiss at her temple. Her blood raced.

She couldn't breathe.

Her nightgown was nearly sheer, not nearly as proper as her cotton gowns. An instant later it didn't matter because it, too, was on the floor.

She kept her eyes closed, allowing him to look his fill. After all, it was only fair. She pressed her palms against her upper thighs, forcing herself to breathe deeply.

"You're beautiful."

She opened her eyes. His face was bronzed with color, his eyes fixed on her breasts. His hands stroked from her shoulders down her arms to cup both her breasts. His thumbs smoothed over her nipples, making them erect.

She bit her lip, managed to restrain herself from pressing his hands against her breasts. They'd always been sensitive and he seemed to know it, taking his time stroking and teasing her.

Finally, he took her hand and led her into the bedroom.

She had never seen a man disrobe as quickly as Bruce. Seconds later he was naked, but this time she could look her fill. She didn't get the chance. He gripped her shoulders with heated palms, brought her forward slowly, his smile visible in the faint light from the sitting room.

Her knees were going to give out any second.

"I should . . ." Her voice faded off.

He slid his hands around her waist, placed them flat on her back and pulled her closer.

"You shouldn't do anything, Ceana, you don't want to do. If you want to leave, you've only to say the word."

She bent her head to look at his growing erection. The sight of him on the beach had given her no clue to how large he was. Bruce was a magnificent specimen of man. She drew her hand over his chest and down his flat stomach. How beautiful he was.

He drew in a breath at her touch.

"Say the words now, Ceana," he said. "A few minutes from now and I won't be able to let you go."

She wasn't a frightened miss. She'd been married seven years to a man she loved. Desire had never been a stranger to her. She knew passion, felt joy in her husband's arms.

Until this moment she'd never thought to feel that again. Until this man kissed her she'd thought to live her life with only memories of those times.

The choice was hers whether to go or to stay. Just as the choice to come here had been hers. He hadn't come to her room. He hadn't cajoled or attempted to convince her. She'd made this decision alone, just as she made the next one to remain.

She looked up to find him smiling again, the expression at odds with the intensity of his gaze.

Her hands trailed up his back, wound around to the back of his neck, pulling his head gently down.

"Kiss me," she said.

How quickly he obeyed.

Take me.

Would he do that as well?

He placed his hands on her waist, lifted her as if she weighed nothing and stretched her out before him on the mattress.

Bending, he placed a kiss on each shoulder. His mouth traced a path from between her breasts before kissing his way up the slope of one to place a tender kiss on one nipple, then the other. He kissed his way down her body to her navel, his tongue darting out to taste her. His hands stroked up her legs, his mouth and fingers meeting at the junction of her thighs.

Suddenly he was kneeling between her legs, his hands beneath her buttocks lifting her for his mouth. When she would have protested, he slowly slid a finger inside her, teasing her even further.

She wanted more. She wanted him to stop. *No, please, never stop.*

She bit her bottom lip to silence her moans as he flicked his tongue against her.

"Please," she said, without meaning to speak.

He didn't answer, only continued with his delight-filled torment.

Tentacles of need spread through her body, each one carrying fire. Her hips arched as she planted her feet on the mattress, arching her hips toward him. Her heart was racing. Her breath was tight.

"Please," she said again.

He only smiled and separated her with his thumbs, another finger gently entering her. She didn't want his fingers; she wanted him. She wanted him to fill her, ease the emptiness.

Her mind scattered as she exploded in a shattering climax of wonder and delight.

Long minutes later she blinked open her eyes.

His gentle smile summoned her own.

She reached up, gripped his arms with her hands and pulled him to her.

He entered her gently. She closed her eyes, startled at the sensation. She wanted him again. Needed him. In moments she was overwhelmed by passion, unable to separate all the various pleasure points in her body.

"Ceana," he said, breathing her name on a sigh as he surged into her.

Her hands gripped his upper arms as the tension built.

Over and over he surged into her, pressing her up against the headboard. One arm reached under her and lifted her effortlessly to him. To her surprise and delight, she climaxed again.

Seconds later he erupted, his cry mingling with hers.

She held him close, feeling his heart beating wildly against her. Turning her head, she pressed her lips against his bristly cheek.

The rapid beat of his heart made her smile, feeling oddly victorious.

Her fingers and toes tingled. Bliss filled her, blessedly deadening the voice of her conscience.

She hadn't meant to fall asleep. Or to wake up cuddled against him, his arm over her waist, his hand flat against her breasts.

His erection cradled her bottom and she knew the exact moment he was awake.

"I have to leave," she said. A hint he shouldn't expect anything further, especially since his erection was growing. She scooted out of the way, her smile broadening when he chuckled.

"It's dawn," he said. "You should leave before Brianag discovers you're here."

The thought of the housekeeper finding her was enough to stop her heart for a second.

She sat up, gathering the sheet in front of her. "You said that just to scare me," she said.

His grin was unrepentant and utterly charming. She ran her fingers through her hair, knowing it was a mess of curls around her head. Her chin was no doubt pink from his night beard, just as there were places all over her body slightly sore from being fiercely loved twice.

Daring herself, she dropped the sheet and walked naked into the sitting room, where she gathered up her nightgown and wrapper. How odd to wear mourning on this beautiful dawn. For the first time in three years something had replaced the yawning loneliness of her life.

The strangest thing was, she wasn't embarrassed or ashamed. She felt well loved, satiated. Satisfied. Well pleased.

He stood at the door between the two rooms. She turned, stretched out her hand, then pulled it back. Words were behind her. Besides, what could she say? She only nodded to him, opened the door slowly and looked both ways. She sent him another glance before she left, closing the door quietly behind her and racing to her suite, hoping she was unseen but not caring all that much if she was.

Some things were worth the price you paid for them. She knew she would always feel that way about this night with Bruce.

Chapter Nine

Macrath was pacing.

That he was pacing in front of her was a sign to Virginia of how distressed he was. Normally, he did everything in his power to prevent her from becoming worried. As if his children didn't do that every single day.

Did it have to do with Carlton? Her son had been suspiciously well behaved for the last few days, but he'd also been cloyingly present. Usually, she had to go in search of her youngest child. Now he was always underfoot. That, too, was odd.

His birthday wasn't coming up, so his good behavior couldn't be ascribed to wishing for an expensive present from Edinburgh. Had Macrath promised him some reward if he behaved himself?

"Were you like Carlton when you were younger?" she asked, not the first time she'd thought such a thing.

The question did exactly what she wanted it to do, stopped him in mid-pace.

He turned and stared at her. "No," he said, his tone disbelieving. "I was working too hard."

"Maybe that's what you need to do for him," she said calmly. "If there's nothing he can do to help you here, maybe Mairi and Logan have duties."

"What do you think he could do, sell newspapers on the corner?"

"Why not? It's better than spending all his time trying to escape Drumvagen, don't you think?"

He looked away, then back at her. "Do you think he's bored?"

She folded her hands calmly and nodded. "I think he's as intelligent as you were, Macrath. I think that's what's at the root of all of this. Give him a job. Give him something to do."

"He doesn't do what his tutor tells him to do as it is."

"No doubt because he finds other things more interesting. How many times have you found him in your laboratory?"

"Too many to count."

"Then have his lessons taught there. Talk to his tutor, see if you can make the lessons have more meaning to Carlton. Instead of learning about Spain and England's wars, what about teaching him about the trade we do with Australia?"

He frowned at her. It was such a ferocious expression, she might've been disturbed had she not been the recipient of its cousin over the years.

"You're much too intelligent for the likes of me," he said.

She smiled back at him. "Only occasionally, my love," she said. "Now tell me why you're pacing."

She reached for her knitting, finding it a wonderful way to focus rather than to stare at Macrath. Not that he wasn't attractive enough to look at every day, but doing so only led to other things. Desire was occasionally unwelcome in the middle of the day, especially with three children and various nurses, tutors, and servants about.

Sometimes Drumvagen was filled with too many people, especially when she hungered for her husband. Therefore, it was much easier to focus on her knitting then Macrath.

"Are you leading up to telling me why Bruce is here?"

Macrath started pacing again. Back and forth he strutted, his arms behind his back, as intent on his progress as the head rooster in their barnyard. Woe be unto those who ventured into his territory without permission. He'd peck you on the legs and fly up and try to batter your face with his wings.

Macrath was just as territorial.

He didn't look at her, which was a clue.

She put down her knitting, watching him.

"I haven't forgotten about Paul Henderson, you know."

That certainly made him stop. He turned and stared at her.

"Did Bruce tell you?" he asked.

She stared at the ceiling, huffed out a breath, then looked at him again. "Really, Macrath, that's almost insulting. Bruce has a very large detective agency. In America. Why would you hire someone to make inquiries in America? There's only one person who would interest you, and that's Paul Henderson. No one had to tell me. I figured it out all by myself."

"Forgive me, Virginia."

"For what? Underestimating my intelligence or for keeping it from me? I think it's two apologies you owe me."

"Very well, you're right," he said with a smile.

"Is he here?"

For a moment she wondered if he would answer her.

"Yes." He threaded one hand through his hair. "We don't know exactly where, but he's in Scotland."

"Is that why we went to Edinburgh? So you could warn Mairi and Logan?"

"Partly," he said. "Partly to draw him out. I wanted him away from Drumvagen."

"The children," she said. Up until this exact moment, she had been relatively calm, but now fear filled her stomach, icing it over. She felt vaguely nauseous and cold.

"He wouldn't do anything to the children, would he?"

"Not if he wants to live another day."

"How can a man be so obsessive? Ten years have passed, Macrath."

He smiled. "The right woman will make any man obsessed," he said.

His look warmed the ice just a little.

"We can't let Alistair go back to school yet. Is that why you've delayed his return?"

He nodded.

"We have to find Henderson, Macrath," she said.

Images flooded into her mind. That terrible time when Paul had drugged her and taken her aboard ship, so close to raping her she'd had nightmares for weeks afterward.

"I want a big knife," she said. "The largest one we have in the kitchen."

At his look, she frowned. "I will not allow my children to be harmed, Macrath. Not by Paul Henderson or anyone. If necessary, I will protect them myself."

He came and stood in front of her, grabbing her knitting and tossing it to the floor. Before she could protest his treatment of her latest project, he hauled her up into his arms and hugged her tightly.

"I love you, Virginia," he said. "From the very first moment I saw you, I think I loved you then."

She closed her eyes and allowed herself to feel comforted and safe, if only for a moment, in Macrath's arms.

Paul Henderson stared out the window of the train, feeling anticipation tingle through him. Ten years had passed since he'd stepped foot on Scottish soil. Ten years, but he returned to this godforsaken country a successful man. A wealthy man who'd come about his riches legally.

People said he was a risk taker, and he was. He had nothing to lose. It was easy to take a bet and double it, be it railroads or silver. His wealth had diversified since he'd taken advantage of America's more egalitarian society. Now he was welcomed wherever he went simply because he was wealthy, not because his father had a title.

In that, he and Macrath Sinclair were alike.

Sinclair's father had been a newspaperman, living close to the edge of penury all his days. While his father had been a chimney sweep, asking no more from life than to send lads up into tiny smoke-filled vertical coffins.

He'd wanted more from the beginning. Now he had it: a private car, a secretary who doubled as a bodyguard, a valet to ensure he was well dressed, a cook who traveled with him. His cabin aboard ship had been a large one and he'd eaten at the captain's table.

No one knew he'd once been a servant in London. Most of

his acquaintances thought there was some mystery about him because he'd let drop certain facts they could gather up together in a loosely constructed story of their own making. He might have been the son of an earl or a duke's progeny. Perhaps he was the illegitimate product of a royal's indiscretion.

All his early self-taught lessons on deportment had served him well. He had the manners and the bearing to be anyone he wished.

Even someone Virginia would admire.

He couldn't forget her.

The one woman he'd wanted, the only one to reject him. All these years, she'd stayed in his mind like a loadstone, an impetus, a motivation to be more than he ever dreamed of being. He would explain it all to her. Virginia, who knew his beginnings, who knew who he really was, would understand better than anyone how far he'd come.

He wanted her. He longed for her. Even when he bedded another woman, hers was the face he saw.

Over the years, his hair had silvered, giving him a distinguished appearance. He was still a young man, with a young man's needs and wants and ardor. He would prove that to her, too.

This time, no one would know he had anything to do with Virginia's disappearance. To that end, he'd interviewed ten likely candidates in Inverness. Three of them were more interested in their payment then their task. Three were so dumb that even after explaining what he wanted done, they still didn't understand. Three were too intelligent, so much so he hadn't even gone into what the task was, for fear they'd report him to the authorities. The last had proven to be a worthy surrogate with a giant's build.

The man would go to Drumvagen and fetch Virginia for him. He'd given the man a detailed drawing of Drumvagen, including the grotto where he could gain admittance to the house. Before leaving Scotland he'd make sure the man went back to Inverness. There was no reason for him to remain in the vicinity or to tell anyone about the nature of his employment.

The other servants—valet, cook, and secretary—knew nothing of the reason for his trip to Scotland, and he intended to keep them ignorant.

He wasn't going to be foolish like he'd been in the past. He wasn't going to concentrate on getting Virginia out of Scotland as much as convincing her of his sincere feelings. Last time, he'd moved too swiftly and scared her. This time, she would know how much he loved her before they ever set sail again.

But first he would take care, seduce her with gentleness, convince her with reason. He would demonstrate to her just how much she meant to him and how unforgettable she'd been all these years.

He wasn't going to resort to force like he had in the past. He was going to take Virginia to his house and convince her, by any means necessary, they'd wasted a decade of their lives. But it wasn't too late. They could still find happiness together. All she had to do was to give him a chance to prove it. He would bring her the world if she wanted it. He could afford to take her anywhere, live anyplace she chose. Her future was not limited to Scotland.

He would take her to his home in Philadelphia, to the mansion he'd built with her in mind. He remembered the town house where they had once lived, and there were certain details common to both homes: the fan light above the front door, the brass knocker, the delicate roselike shade that was her favorite. He'd had rosebushes planted all over the grounds. She would love the home he'd created for her.

His investigation told him she'd had two more children. But they were of an age when they didn't need their mother. She was free now, as free as he was, to pursue the happiness that had eluded them. She would understand, as soon as he had a chance to explain it to her.

He would show her how much he loved her.

By the time they left Scotland she, too, would be regretting the waste of the last decade.

CHAPTER TEN

"It's a wondrous place, isn't it?" Bruce said from behind her. She turned, her skirt twirling about her ankles. He was dressed, but it was evident from his wet hair he'd been swimming.

"I didn't get a chance to admire the grotto the other day," she said, her face flaming. She had been too busy fixated on something else: him. "It's truly a miracle of nature, isn't it?" She moved to stand below the opening in the ceiling. Sunlight beamed down on her, encapsulating her in a golden glow.

When she turned to look at him again, he was studying her.

"What?" she asked. She rubbed at her nose and then her forehead. "Have I something on my face?"

"Beauty," he said.

He mustn't say things like that.

He strode past her, turned and held out his hand. "Come, I'll show you the beach."

She shouldn't take his hand. She shouldn't be lured anywhere with him. Still, she put her hand in his, their palms pressing together. His skin was warmer than hers.

"Where have you been?" she asked.

He smiled. "Edinburgh. One of my operatives thought he sighted Henderson."

Had her question revealed how much she'd missed him the past two days? How much she thought about him? She'd been worried he'd taken off for some imaginary duty to avoid seeing her, but the look in his eyes now proved her fears were ridiculous.

His glance warmed her down to her toes.

"I should run in the other direction," she said. "As fast as my feet can carry me."

"And I as well," he said, smiling at her. "You take my mind from my work, Ceana Mead. I missed you. I wanted to do my duty and hurry back to Drumvagen."

Her heart was thudding so hard she felt breathless with it.

"Did you?"

He nodded.

"Did you miss me?" he asked.

How much braver he was than she.

She nodded.

"Now I'm back, I'm wondering how I'll be able to sleep with your door only a few feet away. Then I think of Macrath and how he's not only my employer, but my friend. I doubt he'd approve of my taking advantage of his hospitality."

His hands slid around her waist. Gently, he pulled her toward him.

"Quite a dilemma, don't you agree?"

Wordlessly, she placed both her hands on his shirted

chest. If she splayed her fingers she still wouldn't reach from arm to arm. How very tall he was, and strong. Look how he'd caught Carlton on the day she first saw him.

He wouldn't come to her because of honor. Would she go to him because of need?

Stepping back, she straightened her skirt, ran her hands down her bodice, fiddling with the cuffs. She really was tired of black, but she would have scandalized her Irish family if she'd chosen to wear any other color.

Once a Mead widow, always a Mead widow.

She would have to return to her life. Or go back to Ireland long enough to explain her desertion and get her daughters. He'd be gone back to America by then and this interlude would be nothing more than memory.

Glancing up at him, she wanted to urge him to stay.

His face was arranged in stern lines, a muscle playing in his cheek. She wanted to touch his full lips, brush her fingers over his mouth. She was enchanted with him, to the detriment of her immortal soul and any sense of decency she once possessed.

She glanced at the passage back up to the library. She really should leave him and take care never to be around him alone.

Instead, she allowed him to spirit her from the grotto to the beach.

The wind was blowing so fierce it made patterns in the sand.

She let go of his hand, turned her back to the worst of it, trying to tame the tendrils of hair brushing against her cheeks.

He seemed impervious to anything nature could throw at him. Standing there, tall and broad, he reminded her of tales she'd always heard of Highlanders.

"Did your family come from Scotland?" she asked.

His bright grin had the ability to lift her heart. How foolish she was.

"I was wagering how long it would take for someone to ask."

"Macrath or Virginia didn't?"

He shook his head.

She studied a rock near her foot. It looked just like a turtle, complete with a tiny little head and pointed tail. Her youngest daughter would have tucked it into her pocket and kept it on a shelf in her bedroom. She bent and retrieved it, brushing the sand away and dropping it into her pocket.

"A weapon?" he asked.

She smiled, shook her head, then said, "No, a present. For Nessa. She likes all things turtle-shaped." She retrieved the rock and opened her palm to show it to him.

He stroked his finger over the humped back.

The moment was too poignant. She couldn't help but think of his lost family and her own darling children.

Of the two of them, she was so much more fortunate. A word she would never have used a few weeks ago to describe herself. But she had a family here in Scotland, and one in Ireland as well. She was surrounded by love and all she had to do was recognize it.

She would have curved her hand around the rock and dropped it back in her pocket if he hadn't suddenly placed his forefinger on the inside of her wrist. Two of his fingers stroked across the tender skin there, as if encouraging her heart to beat faster.

She stared at his broad hand, the fingers callused as if he were no stranger to manual labor.

"Do you hate war?" she asked.

"Another question I've never been asked," he said. "I understand war. I understand the politics that encourages one faction to fight another. I accept it the same way I do cruelty, knowing human nature is not always pretty. But hate? That would be as worthless as hating rain or the cold of winter. It simply is."

"I never thought you a fatalist, Bruce."

"It's my Highlander blood," he said. "To answer your question, my family came from Scotland, from the Highlands. Pushed out by sheep like hundreds and thousands of other Highlanders."

"And they settled in Boston?"

"Not originally," he said. "Canada first and then a branch of the family moved to America."

"Preston isn't a very Scottish name."

"My mother was Moira McElwee. My father's family came from the border. She used to accuse him of being mostly English, while he always said she was a stubborn Scot."

She wanted to ask but was afraid to.

"I lost them both during the war. Nothing to do with the fighting. My father died of heart trouble and I think my mother just willed herself to die not long afterward."

He finally dropped his hand and she returned the rock to her pocket.

"If Nessa collects turtles, what does Darina like?"

She shouldn't have been surprised he remembered her children's names. She suspected he didn't forget very much.

"Animals," she said. "She rescues everything she can find, and there are a great many animals around Iverclaire. Our little cottage is the home of two cats and one very hairy dog. She's nursed an owl back to health and he rewards us by sitting on a tree not far away and hooting all night."

He smiled, then reached out to tuck a tendril of hair behind her ear.

She should have moved away from his touch. She should have told him to keep his hands to himself. Instead, she just looked up at him. Caught by emotion, she was held silent by the need to offer him comfort.

To anyone else he was probably strong and forbidding, but she'd seen through to the heart of him. She wanted to hold him and take away a little of his pain, as he had unexpectedly eased hers.

He took her elbow and guided her close to the cliff where the earth was hollowed out and the overhanging grass provided a little shelter from the wind.

Leaning closer, he shielded her. She placed her hand on his chest, feeling the warmth of him. He was so alive. He was so real, so much a man, surely any woman in his vicinity would be aware of him.

"Will you kiss me?" she asked, feeling brazen and daring.

"Are you tempting me, Ceana Mead?"

She felt like a creature of the wind or the sea, a goddess of either or both. Right at this moment there was no need for earthly laws or social rules of behavior.

She reached up, placed her hand on the back of his neck

and drew his head down. Lifting her face up, she watched as he came closer, noting when his smile faded.

When his mouth claimed hers, she sighed.

What kind of hedonistic creature had she become? To crave the touch of this man, to think about his kisses to the exclusion of any common sense? She didn't care. She entwined her fingers behind his neck, holding onto him because he was a force greater than any wind or swirling sand.

"I want you," he said, lifting his head. "I've wanted you ever since I saw you. I haven't been able to forget the night we were together. I want you in my bed for days on end. If anyone knocks, I'll tell them I'm otherwise occupied. For the first time in my life I'm willing to push aside my obligations. What kind of magic do you hold, Ceana Mead?"

She lowered her forehead until it rested against his shirt. A hollow cavern opened up in her chest. He couldn't say such things, but oh how glad she was he had. He'd given her power with his admission. She was no longer just a widow, a woman to be pitied for her loneliness, but one who inspired lust.

Kiss me again. She didn't realize she said it aloud until he smiled, wrapped his arms around her and lifted her to his kiss.

Take me here against the good earth of Drumvagen. Take me here with the ocean only feet from us, with the lichen-covered stone formations proving this was an ancient place.

Her cries would be silenced by the seabirds above them, by the oncoming rushing tide. Their joining would be as elemental as nature itself.

Instead, he stepped back and shook his head, more in control of his needs than she.

His finger traced a path from the corner of her lips to her temple.

"Ceana."

"Bruce," she said, smiling.

For a moment it felt like the world was held at bay. No past existed for either of them. No future beckoned, filled with responsibilities and obligations. There was only the wind, the sound of the waves wetting the sand, and the cry of seabirds.

Her heart felt squeezed as tears threatened.

She closed her eyes and stepped into his embrace, feeling his arms tighten around her.

Please let her remember this moment for the rest of her life. Never let her forget him and the great gift he'd given her. She was alive. She could feel. She could choose whatever direction her life took her.

Ceana was magic.

She was sorcery and witchery and something Bruce had never before felt. She stripped his mind of every cogent thought. She made him feel, and he'd gone for so long without feeling anything he was raw in her presence.

Kissing her was as necessary as breathing. Holding her in his arms made him somehow feel complete.

Sometimes she would look at him and he was struck breathless by her beauty. Her annoyance made him question himself. Her anger made him instantly defensive. Her passion pushed him to the edge of his restraint.

Every one of her emotions was met by one of his. With her, he couldn't maintain the equilibrium he always had. She wasn't like other women and he wasn't the man he'd always known himself to be when he was around her.

Why had it been so important for him to come to Scotland himself? He'd never even given it a second thought. Once he discovered Paul Henderson had left America, he'd packed his own bags. Not because Macrath Sinclair was one of his best clients. Not because the man maintained an empire and a sufficiently large retainer with his firm. Not even because he wanted to see the homeland of his ancestors. Why had he come to Drumvagen at the exact time Ceana came home?

He might have to believe in Fate.

He wanted to tell her things he'd never mentioned to anyone else. He wanted to lay himself bare and have her judge him, when he'd never cared about other people's opinions before. In the short span of two weeks he had come to look for her, to anticipate seeing her, to thinking of her too much.

When she mentioned returning to Ireland, his mood was affected and his thoughts blackened. He had the feeling once she went back, he would never be the same.

He didn't want to see her wearing black. Nor did he want to be curious about the man she'd married. He envied Peter Mead, and had rarely envied anyone in his life.

Yet she'd come to his room, the greatest gift he'd ever been given. Now she demanded kisses and he willingly obliged, only to be trapped in a net of desire.

How could he allow her to return to Ireland?

For long moments he held her. Then, just when he couldn't imagine ever releasing her, she stepped back.

Her cheeks were rosy, her mouth trembling. He wanted to kiss her again, but if he did he didn't think he could stop.

"Do your daughters have your beautiful blue eyes?"

She glanced away.

"No," she said. "They have Peter's brown eyes. And his red hair."

She looked back at him, placed her palms on his cheeks and studied him intently. "Your eyes are a beautiful shade. Not quite brown. Not quite gold. From the first moment I saw you I thought they were like whiskey in sunlight."

He had rarely been the recipient of compliments, especially from a beautiful woman. He felt his face warm.

She laughed and wrapped her arms around his waist, tempting him to take her right there on the beach.

He bent his head, lay his cheek against her hair, hearing the wind and the waves.

The door to his heart opened, the rusty hinges dissolving as he realized that, despite all the odds, he'd somehow fallen in love.

Chapter Eleven

Carlton was sitting in the corner, reading. Every few minutes he would lick his forefinger and turn the page. Any other day Virginia would have cautioned him that doing such a thing would damage the book, but she was so grateful he was occupied she didn't say a word.

His tutor had gone off to Kinloch village on his half day off, but even if he was still at Drumvagen, it was doubtful Carlton would have left her side. Whatever Macrath told him had made an indelible impression on her son. He rarely let her out of his sight.

A sharp tap on the door frame drew her attention, and she turned to see Ceana standing there.

Carlton looked up as well, then evidently reassured by Ceana's presence, went back to his reading.

He was guarding her.

She was going to have to talk to Macrath, and Bruce, for that matter. This couldn't continue. She had to feel safe in her own home. Even more importantly, her children did not have to guard her.

"Come in," she said to Ceana before turning to Carlton. "Go and tell Brianag we need tea and biscuits." Her son's eyes lit up. Carlton had a well-developed love of Brianag's honey biscuits. She held up one finger. "No more than two, Carlton."

He reluctantly nodded, but escaped from the room.

"You've rescued me from my knight," she said, closing the door and turning to Ceana. "For some reason, Carlton has decided to protect me."

Ceana looked away.

"You know about Henderson," Virginia said, returning to her chair.

"I do," Ceana confessed. "I think it's horrible. I didn't know anything about what he'd done. Nor can I remember him from London."

"I wish I could forget him," Virginia said. "He seems to have formed some type of fixation on me. Come and sit down and we'll talk of other things until Carlton returns."

"I've have a favor to ask," Ceana said, her voice halting.

Virginia put her knitting aside and motioned to the adjoining chair.

After seating herself, Ceana stared down at the black silk of her skirt. "I've not worn anything but black since Peter died."

"And you're tired of it, aren't you?"

"Is it terrible to want to wear something else?"

"No. I can remember feeling the same. Besides, black is only to let other people know you're in mourning. Your emotions aren't tied to the color of the dress you wear. I suspect you'll always miss Peter in your heart."

Ceana nodded. "He was such a good man," she said.

"If you had been the one to die, would he have kept mourning for the rest of his life?"

The question evidently surprised Ceana, because she stared wide-eyed at her.

"I've never considered that. I hope he wouldn't have. I hate to think of him being sad all the time. Besides, my darling girls would need a mother."

"Don't they need a father?"

Ceana smiled. "My brothers-in-law would say they have enough uncles to make up for the lack of a father."

"Do you have enough brothers-in-law to make up for the lack of a husband?"

Ceana's cheeks grew rosy. "They would say love isn't important for me. That I should be happy with the memory of love and want nothing more for myself."

"What do you say?" Virginia asked.

"Can you ever imagine yourself without Macrath and marrying again?"

The thought sent a spike of fear into her heart.

"I don't even like to think of being without Macrath for a day," she said. "But I think he would want me to be happy, whatever that entails. Just as I think Peter would want the same for you."

Ceana nodded, her gaze on the view outside the window.

Virginia stood. "But right now we'll address your wardrobe. I've nothing in mauve, I'm afraid. The shade doesn't suit me. But I have a lovely pale green dress that would look wonderful with your coloring. For a while, at least, you can put your black aside."

Ceana might want to put her mourning aside as well, a thought she didn't voice.

His house was ready for her.

He was ready for her.

Paul looked around the sitting room one last time, gratified his servants had been able to find so many roses. She loved roses. Whenever he thought of Virginia, he remembered her perfume, a soft powdery rose scent.

The rest of the house was sparsely furnished, but it would do. He didn't plan on being here long. Just a week, maybe less time than that.

Perhaps once Virginia was here she'd fall into his arms in relief and joy.

He could almost imagine her words. She'd be so grateful to see him, she'd tell him of her prayers. "All those nights," she might say, "I dreamed you would come back for me."

They might be able to leave for America in a few days. This time he wasn't going to Kinloch harbor. No, he'd arranged for a large cabin aboard a luxurious vessel. They'd board her in London.

"I'm leaving, sir."

He turned to find Connor standing there, filling the doorway.

"You've memorized the map?"

The giant nodded.

"Take care with her. I'll not have her injured or hurt in any way."

"No, sir."

"She has the most beautiful eyes," he said, then caught himself smiling. He shook his head. "Bring her to me safely."

"Yes, sir."

He watched as Connor left the room. A matter of an hour or two at the most and Virginia would be here with him.

What was she doing here in the grotto again? Hoping for another tryst? Hoping to catch Bruce naked again? Hoping for another kiss?

She'd almost gone to his room again last night, halted only by the memory of his honor. Somehow, she had to regain her sanity.

She would leave in a few days and return to Ireland. Peter's family would not understand why she was choosing to move home to Scotland. Something Virginia said the other day had stuck with her. Peter would want her to be happy, and happiness was no longer possible living in Ireland.

She had loved Peter with all her heart and he had loved her, enough to push her away from death and toward life. Enough she could almost imagine him whispering in her ear, "Go, my darling. Seek out your life and live it fully and with joy."

She hadn't done that until coming to Scotland. Once here, she'd forgotten she was a widow and become enthralled with a man.

Moving to stand at the window, she stared out at the beach and beyond to the ocean. The wind was whipping the waves to white caps. Above, the sky was turning gray, the clouds blowing across the sun. She'd missed a Highland storm. Ireland's rains seemed gentle in comparison.

Where was he?

Was he still swimming? He hadn't left a pile of his clothing neatly folded by the door.

He wouldn't be looking for her. He wouldn't be thinking of her, wondering what she was doing.

He would have no idea she'd borrowed a gown from Virginia and done her hair in a different way. Vanity, that's all it was. Foolishness. Could she be so lonely that any man would attract her attention?

He wasn't any man, though, was he?

Passion had erupted between them, shocking her. Passion was heated air and being barely able to breathe, your heart beating so fast it felt like it was galloping in your chest. Passion wasn't one single thing; it was excitement and joy and fear and surprise and delight and disbelief. Passion changed you, made you a different person.

She wasn't the Widow Mead any longer. She was Ceana Sinclair, a woman from a proud Scottish heritage.

Bruce could have been her Highland lover, warrior, leader of men. Gone for weeks or months or years, he would have greeted her the same, marking her as his, so hungry for her he didn't care where they were or who might be watching.

She'd wanted him to take her on the beach, the secluded cove as their chamber. The long grass above them and the earth curving behind them would be their bed. They had no need of perfumed potpourri, not with the scent of the sea and the roses from Drumvagen. With the bright sunlight, there was no necessity for candles or lamps.

Instead, he'd held her close, shielding her from the wind, comforting her without a word spoken. In those moments in his arms she felt herself healing, all the hurts and pains of the past three years fading away.

He'd walked with her to the grotto, bent his head to kiss her one last time. She could see his eyes darkening, the pupils becoming wider. His face was bronzed as he kissed her. Then there was only him and the stars and sparkles behind her closed eyelids.

She hadn't seen him for a whole day. He hadn't been at dinner the night before or at breakfast this morning. Had he left for Edinburgh again or gone farther, to Inverness?

She missed him. When she heard a footfall, she turned with a smile to greet him, only to have a cloth dropped over her head.

Seconds later she was upended.

"**P**ut me down this instant!"

Who on earth was manhandling her this way? Bruce would have had more care. Wouldn't he?

She kicked out, but he only grunted in response. In the next moment he grabbed her legs. She screamed.

"I should have muzzled you," he said.

That wasn't Bruce's voice.

Whoever her abductor was, he was carrying her somewhere. She tried to kick again, but he was holding her so tightly she couldn't. She beat at his back with her fists and he retaliated by slapping her on the bottom, hard enough that she cried out.

"Let me go!"

She could hear his shoes crunching on the sand and felt the sudden bright warmth on her legs. Where was he taking her? Who was he?

Her brothers-in-law were not adverse to force when necessary, even though she'd never known them to use it on a woman. Had they been so upset at her leaving Ireland they'd come after her? Was she being kidnapped in order to force her to return to Iverclaire?

"I don't care how much they paid you. I will not return to Ireland under duress."

Her abductor only grunted in response.

"How much did they pay you? I'll double it."

He struck her again.

Silence was probably a better recourse, at least until she saw her brothers-in-law.

Suddenly, she was flying through the air, landing hard on soft grass. The breath left her in a whoosh. She jerked the covering off her head, and seeing a giant a few feet away, scooted backward on the hill overlooking the beach..

She'd never seen him around Iverclaire. She would have noted such a large man with a pelt of black hair on his head matched by a salt and pepper beard.

Poor man, he really was quite ugly. He had a porcine face, one lined with plump wrinkles. His nose was shorter than it should have been, adding to the piggish look, and his mouth was a little pink rosebud. His eyes, however, were quite spectacular. Green and intent, they sparkled at her like emeralds.

"Whatever they paid you, I'll double it."

He narrowed his eyes, staring at her. Finally, he shook his head, bent down and grabbed her arm. She jerked away.

"I'll walk," she said. "If you put me over your shoulder again, I'll get sick."

He grabbed her arm, propelling her along and forcing her to nearly run to catch up with him. A carriage was parked on the curve of road just out of sight of Drumvagen. After nearly throwing her inside, he closed the door, mounted the driver's seat, and slapped the reins over the backs of the two horses.

Her Irish relatives had a good deal to answer for when she saw them again. If she hadn't been determined to return to Scotland before, she certainly was now.

CHAPTER TWELVE

"The bad man's come," Carlton said, racing into Macrath's laboratory.

He skidded to a stop in front of the long table where his father and two other men were working.

"The bad man's come, Papa, and he's taken Mama."

"Don't be foolish, Carlton. Of course your mother hasn't been taken."

"But she has," the boy said.

"Where did this take place?"

"The grotto." At his raised eyebrow, his son said, "It's still inside Drumvagen, Papa. I didn't leave the house, not until I came and got you."

There was no way to reassure his son he hadn't seen his mother being abducted. Nor did Carlton believe him when he said he'd left Virginia only minutes earlier. There was only one thing to do—prove to his son Virginia was fine. He walked Carlton back to the house.

When they entered the kitchen and Carlton saw his mother, he flew at her, gripping her around the waist. She enfolded her arms around him, pressed a kiss to his hair and looked at Macrath in confusion.

"I saw him," Carlton said, pulling back and looking up at Virginia. "I saw him in the grotto. The bad man took you."

Virginia cupped her hand around Carlton's cheek.

"What did you see, my love?"

Carlton looked from Virginia to Macrath and then back to Virginia again.

"What did you see, Carlton?" Macrath asked.

"A big man with black hair and a beard grabbed Mommy. She had something over her head and she was screaming, but he carried her down the beach."

His eyes sought his father again. "I saw him, Papa. I didn't make it up."

"You thought it was me, Carlton?" his mother asked.

He nodded.

"Was the woman wearing a green dress?"

Carlton nodded again.

Virginia looked at Macrath. "He's taken Ceana."

"What do you mean, kidnapped?"

Bruce stood in Macrath's library. He'd made his base of operations a room on the third floor. When a more truculent than usual Brianag had appeared at the door, he'd not bothered to question her why he'd been summoned to the library. The woman wouldn't say anything, either because she despised Americans or had simply singled him out for her antipathy. From what he'd observed about Brianag, she didn't like many people.

He hadn't expected Macrath to announce that Ceana had been kidnapped.

Virginia looked as if she were going to cry.

"Carlton says he saw who took her."

She reached behind her and drew her son forward. Ever since Carlton's last escapade, trying to clamber up the drain pipe to Drumvagen's roof, the boy regarded him with trepidation. Perhaps Carlton realized his patience was wearing thin.

"What did you see?"

As Carlton related his story, Bruce pulled out a notebook from inside his jacket and began to scribble the details.

"Did you see a carriage or did he walk away from Drumvagen?"

Carlton shrugged. He leveled a look on the boy that had him staring down at the carpet.

"I don't know," he said. "I ran for Papa."

He doubted if the man had simply walked away. "How long ago was this?"

"A quarter hour, no more than that," Macrath said.

He nodded, pushing back his fear. Fear never worked to his advantage. He needed to be cold and calm in order to rescue Ceana.

"She wasn't wearing black," Virginia said. "She wanted to look pretty, so I loaned her one of my dresses."

He concentrated on his notebook, trying to ignore her words. "What color was it?"

"Light green, with a bouquet of flowers embroidered on the fabric in places. Bouquets of pink and blue and yellow. It has a round collar and tight sleeves."

Macrath gently touched his wife's arm. "Bruce is not a fashion reporter, my love."

She nodded. "Of course. Of course."

Her smile was tremulous, more a gesture for Macrath than an expression of genuine humor.

Bruce tucked his notebook back in his jacket pocket and nodded at Macrath. "I'll take the road to Edinburgh," he said. "I think that's the way he would have gone."

"I'll go toward the village."

He shook his head. "No, I want you to stay here. This might be a feint, something to draw you away from Drumvagen. I want you here to protect Virginia and the children."

"Then I'll send some of my men," Macrath said.

He had no objection to that and only nodded. He wished, now, he hadn't sent his two best operatives to Edinburgh. The third man accompanying him to Scotland had been sent to the station to investigate a recent report.

An American matching Henderson's description had been seen on an earlier Inverness train, disembarking at a station not far from Kinloch Village. Where he'd gone from there, Bruce didn't know.

He tried to put himself into Henderson's shoes. If he were intent on kidnapping Virginia again, he would be concentrating on an escape plan. As wealthy as Henderson had become, he could afford to hire a ship.

Before he left the library, he turned and gestured to Macrath, pulling him aside.

"Have your men interrogate the harbormaster. See if any new ships have recently berthed there."

"What do you think will happen to Ceana once he realizes his mistake?"

"It might not be a mistake," he cautioned the other man. "You think he took her deliberately?"

"It's a thought," Bruce said. "He might be willing to trade one woman for the other. Or it's a way to draw you away from Drumvagen."

"I should've gone after the bastard ten years ago," Macrath said.

"You didn't have any legal standing to do so. At least now, once he's back in Scotland, you do."

Macrath looked a little mollified by that. He nodded curtly and went back to stand beside his wife.

Bruce wanted to warn him that sometimes being protective was not enough. You could shelter your family, live a life serene and isolated from the rest of mankind, but bad things still happened. A crazy man appeared; war broke out.

Life changed just when you thought it was safe.

This time, however, he couldn't fail. He couldn't allow something to happen to Ceana. This time would be different.

Before he could reach the door, it flew open, so hard he was surprised the handle wasn't embedded in the far wall.

Brianag stood there, arms folded, chin rigid and eyes blazing.

"They're here, then. The Irish."

He saw a hand reach out and push her gently away. The doorway was suddenly filled with men. To his surprise, two little redheaded girls wound their way through a forest of legs to stand there staring at them.

"I beg your pardon, sir, but is my mommy here?"

One of the three men gently pushed his way between the girls. Taller than the other two, he had brown hair with a hint of red, cut shorter. All of them shared similar features but his were sharper. His nose was longer and narrower, his chin more pointed. His attire was slightly different in that he wore a jacket while the other men were wearing only shirts and trousers and boots that looked as if they'd tromped through a marsh.

Whoever he was, he seemed to be the leader of the three.

"We've come for our sister, Macrath."

Virginia was looking at the two little girls, one of whom appeared to be about Fiona's age.

"Darina?"

The older girl nodded and curtsied prettily. "Aunt Virginia?"

The tears puddling in Virginia's eyes finally spilled down her cheeks as she bent down, held out her arms and said, "Come here, the two of you."

The little girls flew into their aunt's embrace as Macrath moved to stand beside Bruce. To his surprise, Carlton came and stood behind the two of them.

"Is that how you come into my house, Dennis Mead?" Macrath asked.

"It is when our sister deserted her home and her children. She didn't tell any of us where she was going. Nor did she answer our letters once she was gone."

Macrath took a step forward. "She was a member of my family first, Dennis. Would you dispute that?"

"I wouldn't. But I'd like to know why she came to Scotland and left her children behind."

"She didn't leave her children behind," Virginia said. "She came to see her family. She trusted her children in your care."

Dennis frowned at her but didn't speak. Instead, he directed his attention to Bruce.

"This is Ardan," he said, pointing to the man with the red beard to his left. He glanced toward the man to his right, clean shaven with the brightest orange-red hair Bruce had ever seen. "This is Breandan, and I'm Dennis, the fifth Duke of Lester. And who would you be?"

As an American, he wasn't impressed by titles, especially if a man only had to be born to get one.

"Bruce Preston. The man who's going to save her," he said.

He pushed through the three men, shoving at Ardan, almost wanting the man to take a swing at him. He was a damn good brawler when he had to be, and right at the moment he felt like planting his fist in someone's face.

The man let him pass, and he dismissed the three of them from his thoughts, intent on finding Ceana.

CHAPTER THIRTEEN

"What did he mean by that?"

Dennis entered the room fully, coming to stand only a foot from Macrath.

"What did he mean, save her?"

"Someone's kidnapped Ceana," he said.

He explained the situation, the look of rage deepening on the faces of his Irish brothers-in-law. Good, they wouldn't have any hesitation in punishing Paul Henderson, law or no law.

For the first time since he'd learned Ceana had been taken, his mood lightened.

He was torn between wishing to accompany them and protecting his own family. As he turned to look at Virginia, the choice was taken from him. She stood with her arms around Ceana's daughters, her eyes watery and her cheeks still bathed with tears. The sight of her, frightened, brought back too many memories, including the time when her life had been in the balance.

He went to her, wrapping his arms around her, all three of the children caught up in their embrace.

"Don't worry, my love, they'll find her. She'll be fine."

She sighed but didn't answer, and he prayed he hadn't lied.

Bruce was in the stables, readying his carriage, when the three Irish brothers entered.

"We're going with you," Dennis said.

"I'm not going to refuse an offer of help, but there are going to be some rules first."

"And why would that be? You rescue women a lot, do you?"

"I own a detective agency in America," he said. "I work with law enforcement there. I was the one who followed Henderson to Scotland. If you can't agree, then go away."

Dennis finally nodded. After a moment his brothers nodded as well.

Ardan and Breandan helped the driver with harnessing the horses as Dennis stood around looking ducal.

"You're an American," the man said as Bruce came around to the door and opened it.

"I am," he said, entering the carriage.

"You're from Boston, I'm told." The duke entered and sat beside him. A moment later the other two brothers got into the carriage.

"Nearby."

"Would you be by way of knowing our kin? We've cousins in Boston."

"Boston is a big city, Duke. I've never met a Mead before."

"Well, now, you might be looking one up, then."

"I might. Or not." He studied the man. "What I say is the law," he said. "I've a lot more experience in this than you do."

"Where would you be thinking of going, then?"

"The road to Edinburgh," he said.

"A carriage passed us on the way to Drumvagen. In a hurry. Would you care for me to tell you where it went? Or are you all for being the hero yourself?"

He was teetering on the edge of disliking the Duke of Lester, but he nodded.

Ceana couldn't decide if she was angry or sad. How dare her brothers-in-law resort to such tactics to get her to return to Ireland. Had they no sense at all? From this moment on her relationship with them would be forever changed. She would never again look at them with fond exasperation. No, they would be fortunate if she even talked to them after today.

She stared out the window, wondering where the carriage was taking her. To Kinloch Village, she hoped. People loved Macrath in the village, she'd been told. All she had to do was cry out and tell them who she was. Hopefully, someone would intervene.

She focused her gaze on the ceiling of the carriage. It was quite a lovely vehicle, upholstered in pale blue silk. Evidently, her Irish relatives had spared no expense in this abduction.

Would Bruce come after her?

She had wanted her life to change, but she hadn't envisioned kidnapping being a part of it.

When the carriage began to travel up an incline, she wondered if they were nearing their destination.

Please, God, let someone come after me.

She really didn't want to be hauled back to Ireland this way, especially without being able to say good-bye.

Bruce didn't look at the other men in the carriage, ignored their muted conversation, his mind on the task at hand.

Rage filled him, and it had been a very long time since he'd allowed himself to become this angry. This wasn't war; it was worse. War at least had some rules to it. This was one man's obsession, nothing more.

He would always remember the look of fear in Virginia's eyes. Was Ceana feeling the same?

He knew how to catch a thief, how to apprehend a criminal. But how did he handle someone who was insane? How did he reason with someone whose obsession had stretched over a decade and multiple countries?

Let him be there in time.

He felt raw and unprepared. He pushed the emotion away, determined to be a professional. He couldn't afford to let anything deflect him from finding Ceana.

If something happened to her, how would he bear it? How could he look at her daughters and tell them their mother was gone?

He couldn't.

The words would not be said. Even if it took his life in exchange, he would return her to her family alive and unhurt.

"Tell your driver to slow down," the duke said. He stuck

his head out of the window, then said something in an indecipherable language to Ardan. A moment later it was Ardan's turn to stick his head outside.

He nodded to Dennis.

"It's where he nearly hit us, where the two roads come together. I say we go up the hill to the house. It's the first one around for miles."

He hadn't thought of Henderson going to ground. He'd thought the man would try to escape from Scotland just as he had last time. But Henderson might have learned from his mistakes, as most lucky men did.

"The man's a fool if he thinks not to be discovered," the duke said.

"Maybe not as much of a fool as we think," Bruce said. "The place could be well staffed."

"So it's a siege you're thinking of?" the duke asked.

He didn't answer, spoke through the grill to this driver. "Pull off here," he said, then directed his comments to the duke. "I don't think it would be altogether wise to go in announcing our position, unless you have some rifles with you."

"Nary a one, Preston," the duke said. "We thought we were rescuing Ceana from her brother, not from a kidnapper."

"Why the hell did you think you had to rescue her?"

The duke frowned at him, making him appear almost eaglelike. In a few years he would be Brianag's male counterpart.

"She's our brother's widow, Preston."

"Is she not allowed out of your sight?"

"She'd been gone long enough."

The remark pushed his temper up a notch. Now was not

the time to challenge the other man, however. He'd save his anger for Henderson.

They left the carriage halfway down the hill. Bruce spoke to the driver and gave him instructions to turn the vehicle around while he waited. There was every possibility they might have to make a hasty retreat.

He knew the house from his initial inspection of the countryside when first arriving at Drumvagen. When he'd first seen it, however, the structure had been empty. Two stories tall, the house was made of red brick, with a steep pitched roof, white-painted window frames, and a carved front door at the end of a gravel walk.

He hesitated at the edge of the clearing and motioned for the other men to gather around.

"You sure you're not a Scot, Preston?" the duke said after hearing his plans. "I've heard the Scots are sneaky."

"Have you now?" he said in a credible imitation of Macrath's brogue. "I've heard much the same about the Irish. But don't you worry about how sneaky I can be. You just make sure you and your brothers are at the back of the house."

"Ardan and Breandan will be there," the duke said, grinning. "But I'll be right beside you. Ceana needs to see a friendly face when she's rescued, not an ugly one."

He only nodded, but when this was over, he and the duke might be going a few rounds.

CHAPTER FOURTEEN

Ceana didn't know who was more surprised when a strange man opened the carriage door and stared at her.

"You aren't one of my brothers-in-law," she said. "Are you even from Ireland?"

He didn't answer her, only turned to her abductor, standing there hat in hand.

"You stupid bastard," he said calmly. "This isn't Virginia."

In the next moment she realized who he was.

To her surprise, Paul Henderson wasn't unattractive. In fact, he was quite distinguished-looking, with silver hair and a youthful face. His brown eyes held an emotion she couldn't discern. Perhaps it was impatience. Or even casual cruelty, like a man who could run down a dog in the street and not even bother to look back.

When he smiled at her, Ceana felt fear like a kitten's claws traveling up her spine.

"Who are you, madam?"

"My name is Ceana. I'm Macrath Sinclair's sister."

He blinked at her slowly like a lizard. Thanks to Darina,

there were a few in their menagerie at home. All of them looked friendlier than Henderson.

She unpinned her locket and showed him the pictures.

"These are my daughters, Darina and Nessa. They're in Ireland right now, at Iverclaire, where I live. Darina is almost ten and Nessa is seven. I would very much like it if you would release me so I can go home to them."

He didn't say a word. Instead, he flicked a hand at the giant, turned and led the way to the back of the manor house.

She sent a glance toward her abductor, to find him staring at her. A glint of something was in his eyes. Intelligence or compassion? Either way, it was too late for that.

The giant grabbed her elbow and escorted her inside the house.

The kitchen was cavernous and empty, smelling of onions. If Henderson had a cook, she wasn't in evidence. Nor was a maid, from the state of things as they followed him. Dust covered the table in the hall, and the windowpanes were streaked from the last rain.

Henderson escorted her to a sitting room he'd evidently prepared with Virginia in mind. She'd never seen so many roses, all stuffed into vases of every size and description.

She loved roses but the scent of all of them, red, pale pink, yellow, was nearly taking her breath. Her sister-in-law loved roses, but this was a bit excessive.

He turned and walked across the room, rudely sitting in a wing chair before motioning her to the settee.

"Where is Virginia?" he asked.

"At Drumvagen," she said.

He didn't say anything for a moment. "I remember you," he said. "You used to visit her in London."

She didn't recall him, but she inclined her head in recognition of the past.

He flicked his hand in the air and the giant vanished with what she thought must be a sigh of relief. Evidently, he wasn't going to be punished for his mistake, or at least not in front of her.

"I would really like to go home now," she said.

"Would you?"

She nodded. The kitten's claws were digging in.

"I think I'll trade you," he said. "You for Virginia. Would she come, do you think? If she knew it was your life?"

She had been right to ascribe cruelty to the look in his eyes.

"Yes," she said without hesitation. "But my brother would not allow her to."

"So he would rather let you die than surrender his wife?"

"I doubt I would say it as baldly, but yes. He loves her a great deal."

She shouldn't have said that. His face darkened, the easy smile disappeared.

"Don't lecture me on love. I know more about love than you can imagine. I would have given her everything. I can protect her and keep her in a style greater than she's ever known."

"I don't think Virginia cares about wealth," she said. "Granted, it's easier to live when every need you have is answered. But I think she would live with Macrath in a crofter's hut and feel herself blessed."

"Let's hope you're wrong," he said.

"She won't come," she said.

"You should pray she does. Otherwise, I have no use for you."

Didn't he realize how angry Macrath was going to be? Not to mention Bruce. She wasn't wrong, was she? Both of them were going to come after her, weren't they?

How foolish she was being. She must remain calm. Becoming hysterical would not get her out of the situation.

She smiled at Henderson.

"I can see why you would be in love with Virginia. She's a wonderful person and I've been happy to call her my sister-in-law all these years."

He didn't respond, only looked at her with his piercing eyes. She glanced away, noting the other furniture in the sitting room: a secretary, two comfortable chairs in front of the fireplace with a table between them.

Had he rented the house fully furnished? Had he purchased it? Just how long had he planned to kidnap Virginia? Didn't he know Macrath would not tolerate the loss of his wife?

"Would you like some tea?"

She looked at him, surprised. Did he think this was a social call?

"I'd really like to go home," she said.

"Tea?"

He smiled again, an expression not the least bit convivial or amused.

"I should like some very much," she said. If he was insisting on being a polite abductor, who was she to spare him the pleasure?

"And perhaps a few refreshments," he said.

Had he heard her rumbling stomach? Fear or no fear, she was hungry.

She nodded, pasting on an Irish smile. She'd had plenty of opportunities to appear malleable when faced with her brothers-in-law's intransigence.

Better men than Paul Henderson had tried to manipulate her, and they'd failed.

"Thank you," she said. "That would be nice."

He left her alone in the sitting room, closing the door behind him. She heard the unmistakable click of a key in the latch as he locked her in.

Once she was certain he was really gone, she stood and walked to the window. The house was perched on a hill, surrounded by mature trees. Through the branches she could see a view of a glen and the blue haze of mountains in the distance.

She was less than an hour's drive from Drumvagen but it might as well be a continent away.

She'd never seen this house before, but then, she wasn't familiar with the area. She should've come home earlier. She should've brought the girls and visited Macrath and Virginia. Just add that regret to a long list of things she should have done.

Nails had been hammered into the outside of the window frame. Even if she could break the glass, she wouldn't be able to raise the sash. At the moment, however, going through the window looked like her only alternative.

She grabbed the poker from the fireplace tools on the hearth and stuck it under the settee.

Another door sat at the far end of the room. She slowly turned the latch, but it, too, was locked.

A few minutes later she heard a sound outside the door. She raced to the settee and composed herself, calmly staring out the window when the door opened.

Henderson entered the room, followed by the giant now carrying a tray. She wondered if he was assigned to clean the rooms when he wasn't kidnapping women.

He pointed to the table and the other man placed the tray on it. She noted the two bramble berry tarts, her stomach rumbling in anticipation. To her great relief, Henderson evidently had no plans on joining her for tea. After the men were gone and the door locked again, she retrieved one of the tarts.

She was on her second cup of tea when it occurred to her that she should have been wiser. She placed the teacup and saucer back on the tray, staring at the remaining tart accusingly.

Had he poisoned her? Was she going to die because she'd been stupid enough to eat a bramble berry tart? Would she never see her daughters again?

Regret filled her as the room tilted ominously. She grabbed one of the pillows from the settee and lay down before she fell.

CHAPTER FIFTEEN

One thing about the Irish, they knew how to blend into the woods. The duke was no slouch when it came to creeping up on a structure. Bruce barely heard the other man as he made his way around the side of the house. Most of the curtains were drawn, but the ones that were open revealed rooms empty of furniture and people.

He didn't see a sign of Ceana or Henderson. Had the Irish gotten it wrong?

Breandan approached them. "The carriage's here," he said. "It's the same one that passed us on the road."

That didn't mean it was Henderson's, a thought he didn't bother to convey to the duke. If they didn't find anything in a few minutes, he was all for abandoning this location and following his original plan.

He was about to pass the fourth window when he saw Ceana stretched out on the settee.

What the hell had Henderson done to her? He thought he couldn't be angrier, but his temper ratcheted up a notch.

He moved to one side of the window, his back to the house.

"She's not asleep," the duke said from beside him. "Has he drugged her?"

He shook his head. Anger didn't do him any good. He needed a plan. There were four of them, but he didn't know how many men were employed by Henderson.

"He's nailed all the windows shut," the duke said.

"The back door looks the best bet," Ardan said.

Bruce didn't want all four of them rushing the same entrance. Looking up, he gauged the distance to the second floor then studied the oak tree next to the house. He hadn't climbed a tree in years.

"Once I get inside," he said to the duke, "you and your brothers make it through the back door."

The duke nodded.

He swung himself up, hoping the branches close to the window were thick enough to bear his weight. A squirrel chittered at him, evidently upset he'd invaded the animal's domain. Sliding out on the largest branch, he made his way closer to the house. The creaks and groans beneath him made him wonder if he'd make it. It wouldn't be a fatal fall but it would alert the people inside.

He grabbed the windowsill with one hand, pushing the window sash up with the other. With any luck, he hadn't chosen a window in a room currently occupied.

Gauging the distance, he swung off the branch, dangling from both arms. Swimming had increased his upper body strength. He swung his legs up until he placed one knee on the windowsill then pushed himself into the room, turning head over heels until he hit the floor with a thud.

He remained there a moment, listening for sounds of

alarm. When there was no sign he'd been heard, he glanced down at the duke, gave him a thumbs-up sign and turned toward the door.

Now to rescue Ceana.

He hadn't thought to tell the Irish to enter the house quietly, thinking they'd use their common sense and do so. But the duke and his brothers began screaming like banshees the minute they were inside. He could hear them from here.

But by the time he got to the stairs, the three men were in the middle of a melee, fighting three strangers.

He jumped off the staircase, entering the fray, hoping one of the men he punched was Henderson.

Somebody slugged the duke, but other than stumbling backward a few feet, he didn't howl or whine, merely reciprocated with a decent uppercut.

"Which one is Henderson?" the duke asked.

They should have asked Virginia what the man looked like, but he'd been in such a hurry he hadn't thought about it.

One of the burly men with a bloody lip and what looked to be a broken nose pointed to a room at the end of the hall.

"He's in there," he said. "If it's Henderson you want."

Ceana was awakened by two things: the sound of yelling and a slap on her face.

She didn't know who was yelling, but Paul Henderson was slapping her.

"Get up," he said. "Now."

Groggily, she raised herself on one elbow, staring up at him.

"What did you give me?" Why weren't her lips cooperating? How very odd it was taking so long to form words.

He jerked her to a sitting position and then, before she could tell him her stomach was suddenly very upset, he was pulling her to the other side of the room, one arm around her waist, the other encircling her neck.

She kept blinking but the room was still spinning.

Something was very wrong and it was centered on the shouting from the corridor.

The door opened and Bruce stood there, his shirt torn and his lip bloody. She'd never seen a more welcome sight in her life. Her knees sagged in relief.

"Are you Sinclair?" Henderson asked, dragging her backward.

"No," Bruce said, moving toward them. "But you might say I'm acting in his stead. Release her. I've not the patience to ask twice."

The second door opened soundlessly to Ceana's left. She glanced to the side to find the giant standing there. Did Bruce see him? Did she need to warn him?

"I think not. It's Virginia I want."

"You're a fool to try to bargain now. We've subdued your men and you're outnumbered."

She struggled in Henderson's grip. His arm tightened painfully around her neck until she could barely breathe. He really needed to release her before she was sick.

The giant swung back his arm. Suddenly, Henderson crumpled to the floor.

She almost joined him, but Bruce was there holding her upright as the room spun around her.

She was shaking like a newborn colt, holding onto Bruce as she stared at the man who'd both kidnapped her from Drumvagen and saved her. In his hand was a large iron skillet.

"Why?"

"Did you mean what you said about giving me money?" he asked.

There was something to be said for a mercenary man. They were so much easier to understand. Evidently, the giant decided to cut his losses.

She nodded, decided the movement was making her dizzier, then looked at Bruce.

"Have you any money with you? Give this man everything you have, please. I'll reimburse you once were back at Drumvagen."

"Don't be ridiculous." He led her back to the settee while the giant stood guard over Henderson.

The door opened wider and Irishmen flooded into the room. She stared at her brothers-in-law in shock. Why should she be so surprised? Ever since she'd been abducted life had not been normal.

Behind Dennis was Ardan and Breandan, following him as they normally were. The insufferable followed by the inconsiderate and the inarticulate.

"What are you doing here?" she asked.

"We came to bring you home."

"I don't need you to come after me as if I'm a child, Dennis."

"You left Iverclaire without asking us, didn't you?"

"I don't require your permission to live my life, Dennis."

"We'll talk about this when we get home," he said, shooting a glance at Bruce.

"I can imagine Macrath will have something to say about that," Bruce said.

He wrapped one arm around her and she gladly welcomed it, wishing she didn't feel like she was going to faint at any moment.

"I want to go home," she said to Bruce. "Not Iverclaire," she added, frowning at Dennis. "To Drumvagen."

CHAPTER SIXTEEN

Bruce told himself he wasn't a coward. Courage had nothing to do with not wanting to witness the tearful reunion between Ceana and her flame-haired daughters.

He couldn't quite escape it entirely because the squeals of little girls could be heard echoing through Drumvagen.

Macrath would need a full report, and he'd deliver it as soon as the happy reunion was over. He'd arranged for the authorities to take possession of Paul Henderson. The man who'd actually performed the abduction, Connor McMahon, wasn't mentioned when he'd explained the situation. He reasoned that saving Ceana was worth a bit of leniency on his part.

Once on the third floor, he unlocked the door of the room he'd been using as his office. Slowly, methodically, he began to pack away his notes on this case. He'd have them crated and sent to his Boston office, along with the maps and notes he'd made of the area.

He'd remain as long as necessary in order to testify or if the authorities needed any additional information. After that, he would go home.

Go home. Strange, thinking about it—that his big, weathered house didn't feel as much like home as Drumvagen.

Fate had allowed him this time in Scotland but that was all. He was foolish to want more.

"So here you are, then," the duke said.

He looked up from his desk to find Dennis Mead standing in the doorway. Not a good time for the man to make an appearance, not as annoyed and out of sorts as he was.

"For an American, you're not a bad sort," Dennis said.

He only inclined his head, not bothering to return the compliment.

Dennis entered the room, moving the only other chair to a position in front of the desk.

"We'll be leaving soon," he said.

"I'm sure Scotland will be the lesser for it."

Was he supposed to be polite to the man? The duke had been a barnacle on his backside since appearing at Drumvagen.

"It'll be good for Ceana to be back where she belongs," Dennis said, eyeing him closely.

Was this some sort of damn test of his tact and tolerance? If so, he was about to spectacularly fail it.

"Why, so you can make sure she's miserable? What's wrong with her being with her family?"

Dennis reared back on his chair. "We are her family."

"Some family," he said. "You make sure she's still wearing mourning three years after her husband dies. She has to sneak away from Ireland in order to visit her brother. You come chasing after her the minute she's been gone

too long—according to you. Are you sure you're not her
jailer?"

Before Dennis could speak, he added, "I don't think she
should go back to Ireland. Her home might have been there
once, but it isn't anymore."

"And where do you think it is? With you?"

"That's not your decision to make, is it?" he asked.

Or his. Only one person could make it. If he was brave
enough to give her the choice.

Yes, damn it, he was.

"She's no better than she should be," Brianag said, staring at
Ceana and her daughters. "She and the American have been
creeping about at night."

Macrath turned and looked at his housekeeper.

"Ellice was the same," she said. "Each itching to share a
bed with a man."

"I think it's about time you retired, Brianag," Macrath
said.

The older woman stared at Macrath, her eyes narrowing.

"You should take life a little easier. You're no longer a
young woman."

To Virginia's surprise, Brianag only nodded.

What on earth would Drumvagen be like with Brianag
remaining in her cottage in the village? She wouldn't be
stomping about Drumvagen all day, issuing dire pronounce-
ments and Celtic curses.

They all loved the old dear in their way, but Brianag's love was sparingly given and only after a test of wills. The only two people she was certain Brianag adored were Macrath and Alistair. Even she was regarded with suspicion by the housekeeper.

"You'll send for the wagon, then?" Brianag asked.

Macrath nodded. "Whenever you wish."

"Sooner done, sooner over."

She'd never peered into Brianag's room on the third floor and didn't know anyone who had. She couldn't even imagine all the treasures she'd accumulated over the years.

When Brianag left the room, she turned to Macrath.

"Are you really certain you want to pension her off?"

He nodded. "I'm fond of her but I'll not have her scaring Fiona. And I'll not have her telling tales of Ceana."

"Even if they're true?"

"Are they?" he asked, looking startled.

She wrapped her arm around his and headed for the door of the Great Hall, intent on giving Ceana and her daughters some privacy.

"I don't think she's going back to Ireland," she began.

Perhaps it was best to warn Macrath that Ceana might very well be traveling to America.

Two days later Ceana found her daughters and Fiona on the beach, near the window nature had created in the grotto. They were sitting in a triangle, their skirts filled with rocks and sand, their faces pink from the sun, and their hair tangled by the brine-tasting wind.

Bruce sat next to them, perched on a rock as if it had been dragged there to act as his throne.

"Look, Mommy," Nessa said, "Bruce found three more turtle stones for me."

"And he's promised to take me to the barn to see the new litter of kittens," Darina said.

"And keep Carlton away," Fiona added, sending a worshipful gaze toward Bruce.

"You shouldn't be calling him Bruce," Ceana said. "His name is Mr. Preston."

"He asked us to," Darina said, looking affronted. "Didn't you, Bruce?"

He turned his head and nodded once.

He'd made a conquest of the three, that was easy to see. And of her, but hopefully that was less obvious.

Leaving him was going to be difficult.

She pasted a smile on her face and addressed her children. "You need to go gather up your things, girls. We'll be leaving in the morning."

Darina rolled her eyes. Nessa just sighed.

"Why are you returning to Ireland?" Bruce asked. "I thought you'd decided to stay in Scotland."

She glanced at him, taken aback.

"Anything you really want could be sent to you, couldn't it?"

"I suppose it could," she said.

"Are you going only because of your relatives? The duke can be a pushy bastard."

She bit back her smile. "Yes, he can be."

"Don't let him badger you into returning."

"I'm not." Her heart began a thumping beat.

"Then don't go," he said, standing.

"Aren't you returning to America soon?" she asked, leaning against the wall of the grotto. She hoped she looked more relaxed than she felt. She could barely breathe.

"I've thought of expanding my business. I might start a Scottish branch."

"Will you?" Her cheeks were getting warmer, and it wasn't the bright afternoon sun heating her.

All three girls were looking from one adult to the other.

"It seems a worthwhile idea. But for now, I've decided to take a vacation. A holiday, as you call it."

"You mean you're staying here at Drumvagen?"

Warmth raced through her.

"Macrath has invited me to stay. Only for a while, of course. I might be looking for a house to rent. The house Henderson had is not too far away." He studied her. "Would it give you any bad memories?"

What was he asking?

"No. I wasn't there long enough to have incurred any bad memories."

"Good," he said, nodding. "I might rent it. Or buy it if the price is right."

"You're thinking of staying here so long?"

He walked the few feet to her. She ignored the girls' giggles as he grabbed both her hands.

"Life is short, Ceana. We both know how short it can be. I've no wish to lose someone I love again, so I'll be staying as long as it's necessary."

Blinking back her tears, she pulled one hand free and placed it on his cheek, feeling his beard abrade her palm.

She didn't believe in love at first sight. If anything, lust had begun her relationship with Bruce Preston. Yet over the past weeks she'd learned he was so much more than his physical perfection. He amused her. She liked the way he thought and admired his loyalty and his work ethic.

A part of her heart would always belong to Peter, but the rest of her life stretched out before her, empty. It was up to her to fill it with joy and love.

These days at Drumvagen had taught her that lesson.

"I'll court you until you agree to marry me. I'm a very convincing man."

How blind people can be sometimes.

"Oh, Bruce, can't you see I feel the same?"

He glanced over at the girls. "Still, we'll take it slow and proper."

She leaned close to him. "Must we be entirely proper?" she whispered.

Three little girls squealed and giggled as Bruce whisked her into his arms and kissed her thoroughly.

Continue reading for a sneak peek at
New York Times and *USA Today* bestselling
author Karen Ranney's next thrilling novel,

IN YOUR WILDEST
SCOTTISH DREAMS

Seven years have passed since Glynis MacIain made the foolish mistake of declaring her love to Lennox Cameron only to have him stare at her dumbfounded. Heartbroken, she accepted the proposal of a diplomat and moved to America, where she played the role of a dutiful wife among Washington's elite. Now a widow, Glynis is back in Scotland. Though Lennox can still unravel her with just one glance, Glynis is no longer the naïve girl Lennox knew and vows to resist him.

With the American Civil War raging on, shipbuilder Lennox Cameron must complete a sleek new blockade runner for the Confederate Navy. He cannot afford any distractions, especially the one woman he's always loved. Glynis's cool demeanor tempts him to prove to her what a terrible mistake she made seven years ago.

As the war casts its long shadow across the ocean, will a secret from Glynis' past destroy any chance for a future between the two star-crossed lovers?

Available January 2015

PROLOGUE

July, 1855
Glasgow, Scotland

Glynis had planned this encounter with such precision. Everything must go perfectly. All that was left was for Lennox to come into the anteroom.

A few minutes ago she'd given one of the maids a coin to take a message to him.

"I don't know, Miss MacIain. He's with those Russian people."

"He'll come," she said, certain of it.

The girl frowned at her.

"Really, it's all right. Go and get him, please."

She could understand the maid's reluctance. Lennox was an excellent host while his father was away in England. This ball was held in honor of the Camerons' Russian partner, a way to offer Count Bobrov, his wife, and daughter a taste of Scottish hospitality. Hillshead, Lennox's home, was lit from bottom to top, a beacon for all of Glasgow to witness.

She took a deep breath, pressed her hands against her midriff and tried to calm herself. She wasn't a child. She was nineteen, her birthday celebrated a week earlier. Lennox had been there, marking the occasion by kissing her on the cheek in front of everyone.

The anteroom was warm, or perhaps it was nerves causing her palms to feel damp. Her spine felt coated in ice and her stomach hurt.

When was he going to arrive?

She pressed both palms against the skirt of her gown, a beautiful pale pink confection her mother had given her for her birthday. Pink roses were braided through her hair. A pink and silver necklace of roses was draped around her neck, and she fingered it now.

The anteroom wasn't really a separate room but a small area off the ballroom and accessible to the terrace stretching the width of Hillshead. A curtain hung between the door and the ballroom.

They would have enough privacy here.

He'd be here in a few moments. Lennox was too polite and honorable to ignore her request.

Had she worn too much perfume? She loved Spring Morning, a perfume her mother purchased in London. The scent reminded her of flowers, rain, and the fresh rosebuds in her hair.

Her hands were trembling. She clasped them together, took deep breaths in a futile effort to calm herself. She clamped her eyes shut, rehearsing her speech again.

Her whole life came down to this moment. She woke thinking of Lennox. She went to bed with one last glance up at Hillshead. When he called on Duncan at their house, she made sure to bring him refreshments, amusing Lily and their cook, Mabel, with her eagerness. When they met in the city, she asked about his latest ship, his father, his sister, anything to keep him there for a few more minutes. At balls she sometimes danced with him, trying hard not to reveal how much she adored him when in his arms.

The tips of her ears burned and her cheeks flamed. She would melt before he reached her, she knew it. She pressed the fingers of both hands against her waist, blew out a breath, closed her eyes and envisioned the scene soon to come.

She should be reticent and demure, but how could she be? It was Lennox. Lennox, who held her heart in his hands. Lennox, who smiled down at her with such charm it stole her breath.

Lennox was tall and strong, with broad shoulders and a way of walking that made her want to watch him. There was no more handsome man in all of Glasgow.

Suddenly he was there, stepping into the anteroom. Turning slowly to mitigate her hoop's swirling, she faced him.

He wore formal black, his snowy white shirt adorned with pin tucks down the front.

His black hair was brushed straight back from his forehead. Intelligence as well as humor shone in gray-green eyes the color of the River Clyde. A stranger might think life amused him. Yet from boyhood he'd been intent on his vocation, fascinated with anything to do with ships and the family firm.

His face was slender, with high cheekbones and a square jaw. She could look at him for hours and never tire of the sight.

"Glynis? What is it?"

She took a deep breath, summoned all of her courage, and approached him. Standing on tiptoe, she placed her hands on his shoulders, reached up and kissed him.

He stiffened but after a second kissed her back.

She wrapped her arms around his neck, holding on as he deepened the kiss. She hadn't been wrong. She thought kissing Lennox would be heavenly, and it was. If angels started singing she wouldn't have been surprised.

Long moments later Lennox pulled back, ending the kiss. Slowly, he removed her arms from around his neck.

"Glynis," he said softly. "What are you doing?"

I love you. The words trembled on her lips. *Tell him. Tell him now.* All the rehearsing she'd done, however, didn't make it easier to say. He must feel the same. He must.

"Lennox? Where have you gone?"

The curtains parted and Lidia Bobrova entered the anteroom. She glanced at the two of them and immediately went to Lennox's side, grabbing and hanging onto his arm as if she'd fall if he didn't support her.

Lidia was as frail as a Clydesdale. Tall and big-boned, she had a long face with a wide mouth and Slavic cheekbones. Did Lennox think she was pretty?

The girl had been introduced to her as the daughter of Mr. Cameron's Russian partner only an hour earlier. Lidia had barely glanced at her, dismissing her with a quick, disinterested smile, the same treatment she was giving her now.

"What is it, my Lennox?"

My Lennox?

"My father wishes to speak to you." She fluttered her lashes at him. "He mustn't be kept waiting. You know there's something important he wishes to discuss with you." She patted his sleeve. "The future, perhaps?"

Glynis pressed her hands against her midriff again and forced herself to breathe.

Lidia was clinging to Lennox, and all he did was glance down at her.

The Russian woman's gown of green velvet was too heavy for a Scottish summer. Gold ribbon adorned the split sleeves and overskirt and was threaded through Lidia's bright blond hair. Her hoop skirt was so large it nearly dwarfed the room, but she still managed to stand too close to Lennox.

Surely no unmarried girl should be wearing as many diamonds at her ears and around her neck. Were the Russians so afraid their wealth would be stolen that they wore it all at once?

"Come, Lennox." Lidia's voice wasn't seductive as much as plaintive.

The Lennox she'd known all her life wasn't charmed by whining and wheedling.

"Come and talk to my father and then we'll dance. Lennox, you promised. Please."

He glanced down at Lidia and smiled, an expression she'd always thought reserved for her. A particular Lennox smile made up of patience and of humor.

Until this moment he'd never treated her like a nuisance or a bother. Although she was Duncan's younger sister, he'd always seen her as herself, asking her opinions, talking to her about his future plans. Yet now he was as dismissive as Lidia.

She might not be there, for the attention either of them paid her.

Embarrassment spread from the pit of her stomach, bathing every limb in ice. She was frozen to the spot, anchored to the floor by shame.

"Please, my Lennox."

Grabbing her skirt with both hands, Glynis turned toward the curtains. She had to escape now. She didn't glance back as she raced from the anteroom, tears cooling her cheeks.

The last thing she heard was Lidia's laugh.

"Oh, do let the silly girl go, Lennox," she said. "We'll go meet with my father and then dance."

Lennox turned to Lidia Bobrova. He'd known the girl nearly as long as he'd known Glynis, having traveled to Russia since he was a boy.

She smiled back at him, a new and curious calculating expression that made the hairs on the back of his neck stand on end.

"Has the child always been so rude?" she asked.

"I've never found her to be so." Nor would he consider her a child, not the way she'd just kissed him.

Why hadn't her mother noticed the décolletage of Glynis's dress was far lower than normal? He wanted to pull it up himself to conceal the swell of her breasts. Wasn't her corset laced too tight? He'd never noticed her waist was that small.

He glanced toward the door, wondering how to detach himself from Lidia. She'd latched onto him at the beginning of the evening, and from her father's fond looks, her actions had familial approval.

Cameron and Company was in the process of selling their Russian shipyards to Count Bobrov. Negotiations were in the final stage, and he didn't want to do anything to mar them. Yet allowing Lidia to signal to everyone that there was more to their relationship was going too far.

Lidia leaned toward him and a cloud of heavy French perfume wafted in his direction. Her face was dusted with powder and she'd applied something pink on her lips.

He needed to get out of the anteroom before anyone attached significance to his being alone with her. He needed to find Glynis and explain. Then they'd discuss that kiss.

He hadn't expected her to kiss him. His thoughts were in turmoil. He was just grateful Lidia—or anyone else—hadn't entered the anteroom a few minutes earlier.

What would he have said?

She startled me. Hardly a worthwhile explanation, although it was the truth.

He should have pushed her away, not enjoyed kissing her. It was Glynis. Glynis of the merry laugh and the sparkling eyes and the pert quip. Glynis, who had managed to muddle his thoughts tonight as well as confuse him thoroughly.

Lidia said something, but he wasn't paying any attention. He began walking back to the ballroom. Since she'd gripped his arm with talonlike fingers, she had no choice but to come with him.

With any luck, Duncan would help him out, take the possessive Lidia off his arm and waltz with her, leaving him to find Glynis.

He didn't know as he left the anteroom that it would be seven years until he saw Glynis again.

ABOUT THE AUTHOR

KAREN RANNEY began writing when she was five. Her first published work was "The Maple Leaf," read over the school intercom when she was in the first grade. In addition to wanting to be a violinist (her parents had a special violin crafted for her when she was seven), she wanted to be a lawyer, a teacher, and most of all, a writer. Though the violin was discarded early, she still admits to a fascination with the law, and she volunteers as a teacher whenever needed. Writing, however, has remained the overwhelming love of her life.

Discover great authors, exclusive offers, and more at hc.com.

Give in to your impulses . . .
Read on for a sneak peek at six brand-new
e-book original tales of romance
from Avon Impulse.
Available now wherever e-books are sold.

AN HEIRESS FOR ALL SEASONS
A Debutante Files Christmas Novella
By Sophie Jordan

INTRUSION
An Under the Skin Novel
By Charlotte Stein

CAN'T WAIT
A Christmas Novella
By Jennifer Ryan

THE LAWS OF SEDUCTION
A French Kiss Novel
By Gwen Jones

SINFUL REWARDS 1
A Billionaires and Bikers Novella
By Cynthia Sax

SWEET COWBOY CHRISTMAS
A Sweet, Texas Novella
By Candis Terry

An Excerpt from

AN HEIRESS FOR ALL SEASONS
A Debutante Files Christmas Novella
by Sophie Jordan

Feisty American heiress Violet Howard swears
she'll never wed a crusty British aristocrat. Will,
the Earl of Moreton, is determined to salvage his
family's fortune without succumbing to a marriage
of convenience. But when a snowstorm strands
Violet and Will together, their sudden chemistry
will challenge good intentions. They're seized by a
desire that burns through the night, but will their
passion survive the storm? Will they realize they've
found a love to last them through all seasons?

His eyes flashed, appearing darker in that moment, the blue as deep and stormy as the waters she had crossed to arrive in this country. "Who are you?"

"I'm a guest here." She motioned in the direction of the house. "My name is V—"

"Are you indeed?" His expression altered then, sliding over her with something bordering belligerence. "No one mentioned that you were an American."

Before she could process that statement—or why he should be told of anything—she felt a hot puff of breath on her neck.

The insolent man released a shout and lunged. Hard hands grabbed her shoulders. She resisted, struggling and twisting until they both lost their balance.

Then they were falling. She registered this with a sick sense of dread. He grunted, turning slightly so that he took the brunt of the fall. They landed with her body sprawled over his.

Her nose was practically buried in his chest. *A pleasant smelling chest.* She inhaled leather and horseflesh and the warm saltiness of male skin.

He released a small moan of pain. She lifted her face to observe his grimace and felt a stab of worry. Absolutely misplaced considering this situation was his fault, but there it was nonetheless. "Are you hurt?"

"Crippled. But alive."

Scowling, she tried to clamber off him, but his hands shot up and seized her arms, holding fast.

"Unhand me! Serves you right if you are hurt. Why did you accost me?"

"Devil was about to take a chunk from that lovely neck of yours."

Lovely? He thinks she is lovely? Or rather her neck is lovely? This bold specimen of a man in front of her, who looks as though he has stepped from the pages of a Radcliffe novel, thinks that plain, in-between Violet is lovely.

She shook off the distracting thought. Virile stable hands like him did not look twice at females like her. No. Scholarly bookish types with kind eyes and soft smiles looked at her. Men such as Mr. Weston who saw beyond a woman's face and other physical attributes.

"I am certain you overreacted."

He snorted.

She arched, jerking away from him, but still he did not budge. His hands tightened around her. She glared down at him, feeling utterly discombobulated. There was so *much* of him—all hard male and it was pressed against her in a way that was entirely inappropriate and did strange, fluttery things to her stomach. "Are you planning to let me up any time soon?"

His gaze crawled over her face. "Perhaps I'll stay like this forever. I rather like the feel of you on top of me."

She gasped.

He grinned then and that smile stole her breath and made all her intimate parts heat and loosen to the consistency of pudding. His teeth were blinding white and straight set against features that were young and strong and much too handsome. And there were his eyes. So bright a blue their brilliance was no less powerful in the dimness of the stables.

Was this how girls lost their virtue? She'd heard the stories and always thought them weak and addle-headed creatures. How did a sensible female of good family cast aside all sense and thought to propriety?

His voice rumbled out from his chest, vibrating against her own body, shooting sensation along every nerve, driving home the realization that she wore nothing beyond her cloak and night rail. No corset. No chemise. Her breasts rose on a deep inhale. They felt tight and aching. Her skin felt like it was suddenly stretched too thin over her bones. "You are not precisely what I expected."

His words sank in, penetrating through the fog swirling around her mind. Why would he expect anything from her? He did not know her.

His gaze traveled her face and she felt it like a touch—a caress. "I shall have to pay closer attention to my mother when she says she's found someone for me to wed."

Violet's gaze shot up from the mesmerizing movement of his lips to his eyes. "Your *mother?*"

He nodded. "Indeed. Lady Merlton."

"Are you . . ." she choked on halting words. *He couldn't be.* "You're the—"

"The Earl of Merlton," he finished, that smile back again, wrapping around the words as though he was supremely amused. As though she were the butt of some grand jest. He was the Earl of Merlton, and she was the heiress brought here to tempt him.

A jest indeed. It was laughable. Especially considering the way he looked. Temptation incarnate. She was not the sort of female to tempt a man like him. At least not without a dowry, and that's what her mother was relying upon.

"And you're the heiress I've been avoiding," he finished.

If the earth opened up to swallow her in that moment, she would have gladly surrendered to its depths.

An Excerpt from

INTRUSION
An Under the Skin Novel
by Charlotte Stein

I believed I would never be able to trust any
man again. I thought so with every fiber of my
being—and then I met Noah Gideon Grant.
Everyone says he's dangerous. But the thing is
... I think something happened to him too. I
know the chemistry between us isn't just in my
head. I know he feels it, but he's holding back.
He's made a labyrinth of himself. Now all I
need to do is dare to find my way through.

An Avon Red Novel

He said no sexual contact, and a handshake apparently counts. I should respect that—I do respect that, I swear. I can respect it, no matter how much my heart sinks or my eyes sting at a rejection that isn't a rejection at all.

I can do without. I'm sure I can do without, all the way up to the point where he says words that make my heart soar up, up toward the sun that shines right out of him.

"Kissing is perfectly okay with me," he murmurs, and then, oh, God, then he takes my face in his two good hands, roughened by all the patient and careful fixing he does and so tender I could cry, and starts to lean down to me. Slowly at first, and in these hesitant bursts that nearly make my heart explode, before finally, Lord; finally, yes, finally.

He closes that gap between us.

His lips press to mine, so soft I can barely feel them. Yet somehow, I feel them everywhere. That closemouthed bit of pressure tingles outward from that one place, all the way down to the tips of my fingers and the ends of my toes. I think my hair stands on end, and when he pulls away it doesn't go back down again.

No part of me will ever go back down again. I feel dazed in the aftermath, cast adrift on a sensation that shouldn't have happened. For a long moment I can only stand there in stunned silence, sort of afraid to open my eyes in case the spell is broken.

But I needn't have worried—he doesn't break it. His expression is just like mine when I finally dare to look, full of shivering wonder at the idea that something so small could be so powerful. We barely touched and yet everything is suddenly different. My body is alight. I think his body is alight.

How else to explain the hand he suddenly pushes into my hair? Or the way he pulls me to him? He does it like someone lost at sea, finally seeing something he can grab on to. His hand nearly makes a fist in my insane curls, and when he kisses me this time there is absolutely nothing chaste about it. Nothing cautious.

His mouth slants over mine, hot and wet and so incredibly urgent. The pressure this time is almost bruising, and after a second I could swear I feel his tongue. Just a flicker of it, sliding over mine. Barely anything really, but enough to stun me with sensation. I thought my reaction in the movie theater was intense.

Apparently there's another level altogether—one that makes me want to clutch at him. I need to clutch at him. My bones and muscles seem to have abandoned me, and if I don't hold on to something I'm going to end up on the floor. Grabbing him is practically necessary, even though I have no idea where to grab.

He put his hand in my hair. Does that make it all right to put mine in his? I suspect not, but have no clue where that leaves me. Is an elbow any better? What about his upper arm? His upper arm is hardly suggestive at all, yet I can't quite bring myself to do it. If I do he might break this kiss, and I'm just not ready for that.

I probably won't be ready for that tomorrow. His stubble is burning me just a little and the excitement is making me so shaky I could pass for a cement mixer, but I still want it to carry on. Every new thing he does is just such a revelation— like when he turns a little and just sort of catches my lower lip between his, or caresses my jaw with the side of his thumb.

I didn't think he had it in him.

It could be that he doesn't. When he finally comes up for air he has to kind of rest his forehead against mine for a second. His breathing comes in erratic bursts, as though he just ran up a hill that isn't really there. Those hands in my hair are trembling, unable to let go, and his first words to me blunder out in guttural rush.

"I wasn't expecting that to be so intense," he says, and I get it then. He didn't mean for things to go that way. They just got out of control. All of that passion and urgency isn't who he is, and now he wants to go back to being the real him. He even steps back, and straightens, and breathes long and slow until that man returns.

Now he is the person he wants to be: stoic and cool. Or at least, that's what I think until he turns to leave. He tells me good-bye and I accept it; he touches my shoulder and I process this as all I might reasonably expect in the future. And then just as he's almost gone I happen to glance down, and see something that suggests that the idea of a real him may not be so clear-cut:

The outline of his erection, hard and heavy against the material of his jeans.

An Excerpt from

CAN'T WAIT
A Christmas Novella
by Jennifer Ryan

(Previously appeared in the anthology
All I Want for Christmas Is a Cowboy)

*Before The Hunted Series, Caleb and Summer
had a whirlwind romance not to be forgotten . . .*

Caleb Bowden has a lot to thank his best friend,
Jack, for—saving his life in Iraq and giving him
a job helping to run his family's ranch. Jack also
introduced Caleb to the most incredible woman
he's ever met. Too bad he can't ask her out. You
do not date your best friend's sister. Summer
and Caleb share a closeness she's never felt
with anyone, but the stubborn man refuses to
turn the flirtatious friendship into something
meaningful. Frustrated and tired of merely
wishing to be happy, Caleb tells Jack how he feels
about Summer. With his friend's help, he plans a
surprise Christmas proposal she'll never forget—
because he can't wait to make her his wife.

Caleb opened his mouth to yell, *Where the hell do you think you're going?*

He snapped his jaw shut, thinking better of it. He couldn't afford to let Jack see how much Summer meant to him. He'd thought he'd kept his need for her under wraps, but the too-observant woman had his number. Over the last few months, the easy friendship they'd shared from the moment he stepped foot on Stargazer Ranch turned into a fun flirtation he secretly wished could turn into something more. The week leading up to Thanksgiving brought that flirtation danger-ously close to crossing the line when he walked through the barn door and didn't see her coming out due to the changing light. They crashed into each other. Her sweetly soft body slammed full-length into his and everything in him went hot and hard. Their faces remained close when he grabbed her shoulders to steady her. For a moment, they stood plastered to each other, eyes locked. Her breath stopped along with his and he nearly kissed her strawberry-colored lips to see if she tasted as sweet as she smelled.

Instead of giving in to his baser need, he leashed the beast and gently set her away, walking away without even a single word. She'd called after him, but he never turned back.

Thanksgiving nearly undid him. She'd sat alone in the dining room and all he'd wanted to do was be with her. But how could he? You do not date your best friend's sister. Worse, you do not have dangerous thoughts of sleeping with her, let alone dreaming of a life with a woman kinder than anyone he'd ever met. Just being around her made him feel lighter. She brightened the dark world he'd lived in for too long.

He needed to stay firmly planted on this side of the line. Adhere to the best-bro code. This thing went beyond friendship. Jack was his boss and had saved his life. He owed Jack more than he could ever repay.

"Can you believe her?" Jack pulled him out of his thoughts. He dragged his gaze from Summer's retreating sweet backside.

"Who's the guy?" He kept his tone casual.

Jack glared. "Ex-boyfriend from high school," he said, irritated. "He's home from grad school for the holiday."

"Probably looking for a good time."

Caleb tried not to smile when Jack growled, fisted his hands, and stepped off the curb, following after his sister. He'd counted on Jack's protective streak to allow him to chase Summer himself. Caleb didn't want anyone to hurt her. He sure as hell didn't want her rekindling an old flame with some ex-lover.

He and Jack walked into the park square just as everyone counted down, three, two, one, and the multicolored lights blinked on, lighting the fourteen-foot tree in the center of the huge gazebo, and sparking the carolers to sing "O Christmas Tree."

Tiny white lights circled up the posts and nearby trees, casting a glow over everything. The soft light made Summer's golden hair shine. She smiled with her head tipped back, her bright blue eyes glowing as she stared at the tree.

His temper flared when the guy hooked his arm around her neck and pulled her close, nearly spilling his beer down the front of her. She laughed and playfully shoved him away. The guy smiled and put his hand to her back, guiding her toward everyone's favorite bar. Several other people joined their small group.

Caleb tapped Jack's shoulder and pointed to Summer's back. Her long hair was bundled into a loose braid he wanted to unravel and then run his fingers through the silky strands.

"There she goes."

"What the . . . Let's go get her."

Caleb grabbed Jack's shoulder. "If you go in there and demand she leaves, it'll only embarrass her in front of all her friends. Let's scout the situation. Lie low."

"You're right. She'll only fight harder if we demand she come home. Let's get a beer."

Caleb grimaced. Hell yes, he wanted to drag Summer home, but fought the compulsion.

He did not want to watch her with some other guy.

Why did he torture himself like this?

An Excerpt from

THE LAWS OF SEDUCTION
A French Kiss Novel
by Gwen Jones

In the final fun and sexy French Kiss novel,
sparks fly as sassy lawyer Charlotte Andreko
and Rex Renaud, the COO of Mercier
Shipping, race to clear his name after he's
arrested for a crime he didn't commit.

In her fifteen years as an attorney, Charlotte had never let anyone throw her off her game, and she wasn't about to let it happen now.

So why was she shaking in her Louboutins?

"Put your briefcase and purse on the belt, keys in the tray, and step through," the officer said, waving her into the metal detector.

She complied, cold washing through her as the gate behind her clanged shut. She glanced over her shoulder, thinking how much better she liked it when her interpretation of "bar" remained figurative.

"Name . . . ?" asked the other cop at the desk.

"Charlotte Andreko."

He ran down the list, checking her off, then held out his hand, waggling it. "Photo ID and attorney card."

She grabbed her purse from the other side of the metal detector and dug into it, producing both. After the officer examined them, he sat back with a smirk. "So you're here for that Frenchie dude, huh? What's he—some kinda big deal?"

She eyed him coolly, hefting her briefcase from the belt. "They're all just clients to me."

"That so?" He dropped his gaze, fingering her IDs. "How come he don't have to sit in a cell? Why'd he get a private room?"

Why are you scoping my legs, you big douche? "It's your jail. Why'd you give him one?"

He cocked a brow. "You're pretty sassy, ain't you?"

"And you're wasting my time," she said, swiping back her IDs. *God, it's times like these I really hate men.* "Are you going to let me through or what?"

He didn't answer. He just leered at her with that simpering grin as he handed her a visitor's badge, reaching back to open the next gate.

"Thank you." She clipped it on, following the other cop to one more door at the other side of the vestibule.

"It's late," the officer said, pressing a code into a keypad, "so we can't give you much time."

"I won't need much." After all, how long could it take to say *no fucking way?*

"Then just ring the buzzer by the door when you're ready to leave." When he opened the door and she stepped in, her breath immediately caught at the sight of the man behind it. She clutched her briefcase so tightly she could feel the blood rushing from her fingers.

"*Bonsoir*, Mademoiselle Andreko," Rex Renaud said.

Even with his large body cramped behind a metal table, the Mercier Shipping COO had never looked more imposing—

and, in spite of his circumstances, never more elegant. The last time they'd met had been in Boston, negotiating the separation terms of his company's lone female captain, Dani Lloyd, who had recently become Marcel Mercier's wife. With his cashmere Kiton bespoke now replaced by Gucci black tie, he struck an odd contrast in that concrete room, yet still exuded a coiled and barely contained strength. He folded his arms across his chest as his black eyes fixed on hers, Charlotte getting the distinct impression he more or less regarded her as cornered prey.

All at once the door behind her slammed shut, and her heart beat so violently she nearly called the officer back. Instead she planted her heels and forced herself to focus, staring the Frenchman down. "All right, I'm here," she said *en français*. "Not that I know why."

If there was anything she remembered about Rex Renaud—and he wasn't easy to forget—it was how lethally he wielded his physicality. How he worked those inky eyes, jet-black hair and Greek-statue handsomeness into a kind of immobilizing presence, leaving her weak in the knees every time his gaze locked on hers. Which meant she needed to work twice as hard to keep her wits sharp enough to match his, as no way would she allow him the upper hand.

An Excerpt from

SINFUL REWARDS 1
A Billionaires and Bikers Novella
by Cynthia Sax

Belinda "Bee" Carter is a good girl; at least, that's
what she tells herself. And a good girl deserves
a nice guy—just like the gorgeous and moody
billionaire Nicolas Rainer. Or so she thinks,
until she takes a look through her telescope
and sees a naked, tattooed man on the balcony
across the courtyard. He has been watching
her, and that makes him all the more enticing.
But when a mysterious and anonymous text
message dares her to do something bad, she
must decide if she is really the good girl she has
always claimed to be, or if she's willing to risk
everything for her secret fantasy of being watched.

An Avon Red Novella

I'd told Cyndi I'd never use it, that it was an instrument purchased by perverts to spy on their neighbors. She'd laughed and called me a prude, not knowing that I was one of those perverts, that I secretly yearned to watch and be watched, to care and be cared for.

If I'm cautious, and I'm always cautious, she'll never realize I used her telescope this morning. I swing the tube toward the bench and adjust the knob, bringing the mysterious object into focus.

It's a phone. Nicolas's phone. I bounce on the balls of my feet. This is a sign, another declaration from fate that we belong together. I'll return Nicolas's much-needed device to him. As a thank you, he'll invite me to dinner. We'll talk. He'll realize how perfect I am for him, fall in love with me, marry me.

Cyndi will find a fiancé also—everyone loves her—and we'll have a double wedding, as sisters of the heart often do. It'll be the first wedding my family has had in generations.

Everyone will watch us as we walk down the aisle. I'll wear a strapless white Vera Wang mermaid gown with organza and lace details, crystal and pearl embroidery accents, the bodice fitted, and the skirt hemmed for my shorter height. My hair will be swept up. My shoes—

Voices murmur outside the condo's door, the sound piercing my delightful daydream. I swing the telescope upward, not wanting to be caught using it. The snippets of conversation drift away.

I don't relax. If the telescope isn't positioned in the same way as it was last night, Cyndi will realize I've been using it. She'll tease me about being a fellow pervert, sharing the story, embellished for dramatic effect, with her stern, serious dad—or, worse, with Angel, that snobby friend of hers.

I'll die. It'll be worse than being the butt of jokes in high school because that ridicule was about my clothes and this will center on the part of my soul I've always kept hidden. It'll also be the truth, and I won't be able to deny it. I am a pervert.

I have to return the telescope to its original position. This is the only acceptable solution. I tap the metal tube.

Last night, my man-crazy roommate was giggling over the new guy in three-eleven north. The previous occupant was a gray-haired, bowtie-wearing tax auditor, his luxurious accommodations supplied by Nicolas. The most exciting thing he ever did was drink his tea on the balcony.

According to Cyndi, the new occupant is a delicious piece of man candy—tattooed, buff, and head-to-toe lickable. He was completing armcurls outside, and she enthusiastically counted his reps, oohing and aahing over his bulging biceps, calling to me to take a look.

I resisted that temptation, focusing on making macaroni and cheese for the two of us, the recipe snagged from the diner my mom works in. After we scarfed down dinner, Cyndi licking her plate clean, she left for the club and hasn't returned.

Three-eleven north is the mirror condo to ours. I

straighten the telescope. That position looks about right, but then, the imitation UGGs I bought in my second year of college looked about right also. The first time I wore the boots in the rain, the sheepskin fell apart, leaving me barefoot in Economics 201.

Unwilling to risk Cyndi's friendship on "about right," I gaze through the eyepiece. The view consists of rippling golden planes, almost like . . .

Tanned skin pulled over defined abs.

I blink. It can't be. I take another look. A perfect pearl of perspiration clings to a puckered scar. The drop elongates more and more, stretching, snapping. It trickles downward, navigating the swells and valleys of a man's honed torso.

No. I straighten. This is wrong. I shouldn't watch our sexy neighbor as he stands on his balcony. If anyone catches me . . .

Parts 1, 2, 3, 4, and 5 available now!

An Excerpt from

SWEET COWBOY CHRISTMAS
A Sweet, Texas Novella
by Candis Terry

Years ago, Chase Morgan gave up his Texas life
for the fame and fortune of New York City, and
he never planned on coming back—especially
not for Christmas. But when his life is turned
upside down, he finds himself at the door of sexy
Faith Walker's Magic Box Guest Ranch. Chase is
home for Christmas, and it's never been sweeter.

Chase had come up to stand beside her and hand her more ornaments. While most of the influential men who visited the ranch usually reeked of overpowering aftershave, Chase wore the scent of warm man and clean cotton. Tonight, when he'd shown up in a pair of black slacks and a black T-shirt, she'd had to find a composure that had nothing to do with his rescuing her.

She'd taken a fall all right.

For him.

Broken her own damn rules is what she'd done. Hadn't she learned her lesson? Men with pockets full of change they threw around like penny candy at a parade weren't the kind she could ever be interested in.

At least never again.

Trouble was, Chase Morgan was an extremely sexy man with bedroom eyes and a smile that said he could deliver on anything he'd promise in that direction. Broad shoulders that confirmed he could carry the weight of the world if need be. And big, capable hands that had already proven they could catch her if she fell.

He was trouble.

And she had no doubt she was in trouble.

Best to keep to the subject of the charity work and leave the drooling for some yummy, untouchable movie star like Chris Hemsworth or Mark Wahlberg.

Discreetly, she moved to the other side of the tree and hung a pinecone Santa on a higher branch. "We also hold a winter fund-raiser, which is what I'm preparing for now."

"What kind of fund-raiser?" he asked from right beside her again, with that delicious male scent tickling her nostrils.

"We hold it the week before Christmas. It's a barn dance, bake sale, auction, and craft fair all rolled into one." She escaped to the other side of the tree, but he showed up again, hands full of dangling ornaments. "Last year we raised $25,000. I'd like to top that this year if possible."

"You must have a large committee to handle all that planning."

She laughed.

Dark brows came together over those green eyes that had flashes of gold and copper near their centers. "So I gather you're not just the receptionist-slash–tree decorator."

"I have a few other talents I put to good use around here."

"Now you've really caught my interest."

To get away from the intensity in his gaze, she climbed up the stepstool and placed a beaded-heart ornament on the tree. She could only imagine how he probably used that intensity to cut through the boardroom bullshit.

As a rule, she never liked the clientele to know she was the sole owner of the ranch. Even though society should be living in this more open-minded century, there were those who believed it was still a man's world.

"Oh, it's really nothing that special," she said. "Just some odds and ends here and there."

When she came down the stepstool, his hands went to her waist to provide stability. At least that's what she told herself, even after those big warm palms lingered when she'd turned around to face him.

"Fibber," he said while they were practically nose to nose.

"I beg your pardon?"

"You know what I do for a living, Faith? How I've been so successful? I read people. I come up with an idea, then I read people for how they're going to respond. Going into a pitch, I know whether they're likely to jump on board or whether I need to go straight to plan B."

His grip around her waist tightened, and the fervor with which he studied her face sent a shiver racing down her spine. There was nothing threatening in his eyes or the way his thumbs gently caressed the area just above the waistband of her Wranglers.

Quite the opposite.

"You have the most expressive face I've ever seen," he declared. "And when you're stretching the truth, you can't look someone in the eye. Dead giveaway."

"And you've known me for what? All of five minutes?" she protested.

One corner of his masculine lips slowly curved into a smile. "Guess that's just me being presumptuous again."

Everything female in Faith's body awakened from the death sleep she'd put it in after she'd discovered the man she'd been just weeks away from marrying, hadn't been the man she'd thought him to be at all.

"Looks like we're both a little too trigger-happy in the jumping-the-gun department," she said, while deftly extricating herself from his grasp even as her body begged her to stay put.

"Maybe."

Backing away, she figured she'd tempted herself enough for one night. Best they get dinner over with before she made some grievous error in judgment she'd never allow herself to forget.

She clapped her hands together. "So . . . how about we get to that dinner?"

"Sounds great." His gaze wandered all over her face and body. "I'm getting hungrier by the second."

Whoo boy.